TOTES MEER

Dai Vaughan, one of the most imperiously intelligent fiction-writers alive, has constructed a novel of complete originality ... This is a book to keep, to re-read and to give. – *Neal Ascherson*

TOTES MEER

DAI VAUGHAN

seren

Seren is the book imprint of
Poetry Wales Press Ltd
Nolton Street, Bridgend, CF31 3BN, Wales
www.seren-books.com

ISBN 1-85411-338-0

A CIP record for this title is available from
the British Library

The publisher works with the financial assistance of the
Welsh Books Council

Printed in Plantin by CPD Wales, Ebbw Vale

Explanation

When the London Tate Gallery bifurcated, I paid a visit to what was now Tate Britain to see what treasures might have been excavated from their cellars to fill the newly available space. In fact at that point there were few; but one painting to which my eye was drawn – though scarcely a forgotten item – was Paul Nash's Totes Meer, his rendering of the field at Cowley, near Oxford, which served during World War II as a graveyard for crashed Nazi aircraft.

A waning moon hangs over this grey-green sea whose surf-line, so to speak, reaches from the left foreground towards the right background. The occasional split cross on wing-tip or fuselage hints at a resemblance to toppled tombstones. All is seemingly motionless until we notice, far to the right, a white owl which flaps away low across the wreckage as a gull will skim low over waves. This bird, the only sign of life amid the lunar desolation, is effectively camouflaged by its continuing the faint glimmer of the rim of a cloudbank; and in any case it is about to leave the picture. The composition is held in equilibrium by a subtle interplay of shapes: the arc of the owl's wings echoing the slice of the moon, the moon's faintly-seen roundness in turn echoed in a prominent wheel and, elsewhere, reversed in the black void of an empty wheel-housing. The bracket of the wheel, near to the foreground, is painted a light blue which, intrusive as a discord, animates this otherwise almost gothic scene with the sting of modernity.

The achievement of the picture as propaganda lay in its absorbing the machineries of threat and destruction into the dream landscape of Nash's England – a landscape already, for those who know it, cryptic with time-scarred signs. In terms of Nash's own iconography, there must have been a doubling of mortality in the representation of wrecked aircraft as a Dead Sea, since – according to his posthumous essay 'Aerial Flowers' – he had always understood flight itself as a metaphor for death.

As I lingered before Totes Meer at the Tate, it struck me with the force of a certainty that I had first seen it in the War Artists' exhibition at the National Gallery. This was the exhibition filmed in 1941 for the documentary *Listen to Britain* – though the occasion when I was taken there by my father would have been a year or two later, probably 1943. Of course, I have seen the painting more than once in the intervening years. My sudden recollection of this putative first instance may have been prompted by my having recently had occasion to view *Listen to Britain* again. But the paint on the canvas – and therefore, by transference, on the German aircraft – seemed as fresh now as when I had encountered it for the first time.

The present work of fiction contains little reference to the war; and it may therefore seem odd – even, to some, impertinent – that I should choose to call it *Totes Meer*. But the title is intended less as an indication of content than as a form of dedication, an act of homage. The startling experience of temporal elision, of the bridging of the ineradicable years, of the shocking superimposition of youth upon age: it was this which led me to borrow for my book the title of Nash's painting.

A Rabbit

I

Dear Mum and Dad,

Half way through the holiday, and I'm just writing to let you know how the first week has gone.

The journey was very comfortable, and I didn't feel sick at all. Auntie Gwen took me to the restaurant car, which is the first time I've ever been in one, and the food was very good. The most striking thing was after leaving the rolling green fields of England, to come out of the Severn tunnel and see grey grass sweeping up at either side to a threatening procession of telegraph poles. So all you saw at first of Wales was grey clouds. Something else I noticed was that, whereas horses in English fields are always standing up, here they lie down if they feel like it.

We quickly settled in, and Auntie Martha has made us feel really at home except for the one or two little difficulties one always finds in a strange place, such as where and when to clean one's shoes. There are sides of bacon hanging from the beams in the living room to be 'cured' (of what?), and you have to dodge around them so as not to bump your head. The rationing can't have been much of a problem. I don't quite know what I ought to call Auntie Martha's husband, as she always just addresses him as Pritchard. That must be with her having known him such a long time before she married him. But I feel it would sound a bit rude to call him that, and he's a bit too distantly related to be called Uncle, so I rather finish up not calling him anything. A few days after we arrived, I was woken in the middle of the night by a lot of urgent movement and a sickly smell from downstairs, and it turned out they were boiling treacle to treat a cow that was suffering from redwater – whatever that is. But actually they don't keep many cows nowadays, and Pritchard makes his living mainly running people about in his car.

The weather has been unsettled, and sometimes heavy rain has kept us indoors playing games of rummy – which I usually lose. But we've managed nevertheless to pay visits to lots of people Auntie Gwen knows because she comes here so often, who can mostly claim to be relatives of some sort, and even when we go into the Post Office for half a dozen stamps we get invited in for tea and cakes. On our third day, we all went on a long trip to visit an Uncle Idris and Auntie Mai. After tea, while the women were talking, Uncle took me out to show me his fields on the hillside behind the house. These two rather weedy fields were obviously his pride and joy, but I didn't know what to say to him about them. (What is there to say about two small fields?) I got a funny feeling that, if I'd said the right things, he'd have burst into tears and spread his arms wide and exclaimed, "They're yours when I am gone!"

More rummy when we went to see Auntie Gwen's friend Olwen, who until recently was a missionary in Rhodesia, and told us about some village in the middle of the bush where the local shop had a shelf stacked with canisters of Whittaker and Gumthorpe's Superior Ballroom Chalk – By Appointment to King Edward VII. She's now working till her retirement as a teacher at the local elementary school, and showed us stories written by some of her pupils. We had a good laugh at lines like, "Then St George galloped up on a house..." but in all honesty I couldn't help feeling their efforts were a good deal more imaginative than anything I could have produced at their age.

The people at the Post Office have a son called Bidge, a kindly boy though a bit uncouth, who took me up the mountain yesterday evening to shoot rabbits. Well, actually he shot the rabbits and I kept missing and frightening them off, so that we had to wait for them to reassemble before he could shoot another. I expect I'll get better at it when I'm on

National Service, but for the moment I felt a bit inadequate.

Anyhow, I think that's about it for the moment. I dare say I'll have more to tell you when we get back.

Give Shambles my love...

II

FRIDAY 18 MAY

Settling in at the farm after yesterday's long rail journey. It was a dramatic moment when we emerged from the tunnel between grey-green grassy sides of a cutting which swept up wide and high to a relentless procession of black telegraph poles, only a dismal grey arch of sky above, and alongside the tracks some railwaymen turned to glower almost accusingly at the passing train.

Auntie Martha's husband Pritchard picked us up from the station, and I noticed in the distance as we passed it the cluster of very big rocks on a mountain top which I remember from when I came here as a small child, and which is called Garn Fawr (at least, I assume that's how you spell it). One wonders how they got there, because they don't look man-made, and yet one can't quite imagine a retreating glacier having plonked such huge stones right on the very top like that.

Auntie Martha's old father, who wears a cap all the time and mostly sits on a settle by the fire, doesn't speak English, or at any rate is shy of doing so in front of native English speakers. But he talks very softly with a voice like a brook rippling over stones, which is very beautiful. The house seems very traditional, and there are sides of bacon hanging from the beams which remind me of some other idea, perhaps of men swinging from a gibbet, especially when they've been bumped in passing and sway a little, or perhaps it's hammocks hanging below decks in a ship. I believe they've had salt rubbed into them as a preservative. Or perhaps it's saltpetre, I'm not sure.

Auntie Gwen has had to do the rounds of all the people who would be offended if she didn't, and has taken me with

her, and we have spent almost all our time indoors in somebody's house or another's, and I have been a long time in
hot, stuffy rooms drinking tea. I've ended up with quite a
headache. I hope we'll be able to go off on a proper walk
tomorrow. Even at the Post Office, where we went just to
buy a dozen stamps, we were invited in for a cup of tea and
cakes. Mrs Evans has a son called Bidge (presumably not
his real name), and she said that when he came home she'd
suggest to him that he take me one evening to shoot rabbits,
and that he'd probably phone to arrange when. I don't
think I really fancy that, and was quite relieved when the
evening passed without his ringing. Perhaps she forgot to
say anything. I rather hope so. We spent the evening playing
cards, which I find rather boring, but it's assumed that I
enjoy it because I used to when I was younger – and I don't
like to say anything. Besides, there's not much else to do.

But I really must try and have the self-discipline to write
up my diary every evening. If I let it lapse, then my descen-
dants will have no idea who I was. That sounds pretentious,
I expect, but really it isn't, because if your thoughts and
experiences are not going to survive you, you may as well
never have lived.

MONDAY 21 MAY

Two days since I've found time to do my diary. It's all this
visiting that's to blame. On Saturday we went to see Auntie
Gwen's old friend Olwen, who used to be a missionary. We
played cards, and she told us stories about Rhodesia, and
then in the evening two of Olwen's cousins turned up, and
we stood around the piano as she played excerpts from 'The
Messiah'. We were all expected to join in singing, but the
words were in Welsh, and I couldn't read them quickly

enough, so I think the others were all left with the impression I couldn't sing, which was a bit mortifying.

Then yesterday Pritchard took us in his car to visit Uncle Idris and Auntie Mai. As Auntie Mai was putting out the cakes, she said, "Help yourself, just as if you were at home" – to which Uncle added, "Only don't eat so much." After tea, as the others were talking, he took me out to show me his fields, but I was not sure what conclusion I was supposed to draw from them. It was obviously important to him, though, to show them to someone, and when I left it was with the awful sense of having hurt his feelings yet not understanding how or why. On the way back we passed close to the mountain with Garn Fawr at the top, and as I turned to look, a shaft of silver sunlight fell upon it out of a tumble of grey clouds, and I noticed the cracks on its face in the form of a diagonal cross, and I was suddenly reminded of a seated, impassive figure of the Buddha. (I must look into Buddhism one of these days.)

I've decided, actually, that I'll try to write a short story about Garn Fawr, or at least with Garn Fawr as some sort of brooding and perhaps benevolent presence above the action. I haven't decided yet what it will be about, but I bought a little exercise book at the Post Office in which I've already started to make notes for it.

Last night, at about two o'clock, I was woken by the sound of urgent activity and voices downstairs, and the house was pervaded by a heavy, dark sweet smell, an almost physical stickiness in the atmosphere as one breathed it. When we came down this morning – a bit like guests at a hotel, it suddenly struck me – they told us that one of the cows had been suffering from 'red-water', and that they'd had to prepare a treacle drench for it. I didn't inquire into the details, but I did remember having heard a lot of plaintive mooing in the small hours.

This realisation that we're not, either of us, really part of what happens in this house makes me feel somehow closer to Auntie Gwen. Actually I've been noticing since we came here that, whereas in other company she always seems to want to keep control of the situation by being aloof and using a lot of sarcasm, she doesn't behave that way here at all, and I'm beginning to feel a great warmth towards her. I don't know quite what I mean by that. But my heart certainly gave a great thump when I heard that someone from the village had mistaken us for a married couple. Auntie Gwen must be at least 35, and although she still looks young, I was surprised that anyone could make that mistake.

Today, because it was warm and sunny and because all the necessary visits appear to have been made (at least for the moment), the two of us went for a long walk and tried to find a path leading up to Garn Fawr. But we couldn't, so we went on to a clifftop overlooking a bay. The grass was dry enough for us to sit on for a while and read. Auntie Gwen was wearing a yellow floral summer dress, and as she lowered herself I glimpsed the under-surface of her thigh. She had no stockings on, and it reminded me of the colour of a plane tree bough from which the bark has been stripped. I felt guilty for having looked, yet at the same time wished I could have feasted my eyes for longer. Eventually, to avoid the compulsion to keep glancing at her legs, I went and clambered among the rocks until it was time to go.

On the way home, Auntie Gwen payed great attention to the wildflowers which are beginning to show themselves in the hedgerows, whilst I was more interested in the rocks and in the wide selection of greys in this landscape. An old chapel we passed was built of stone blocks varying between green-grey and orange-grey, and covered in places with yellow lichen. Or perhaps I mean algae. Are those just two different words for the same thing? Neither of us knew for sure, and even to share this ignorance, I felt, brought us closer together. Then we got caught in a freak shower, and took shelter in a narrow cleft in the rock alongside the lane. I felt a strong desire to put my arm around Auntie Gwen. But I didn't dare. And yet at the same time, again, I felt ashamed of not daring. Ashamed both ways. So what am I truly?

However, I must try hard to rid my mind of those moments. Tonight I shall have to stuff my pyjama bottoms with spare underclothing. I'm afraid of having a wet dream, and it would be terrible for that to happen in someone else's bed, where I haven't the wherewithal for dealing with it.

WEDNESDAY 23 MAY

This afternoon, just when I'd forgotten all about it, we got the phone call from Bidge. We were to meet at the Post Office at 6 o'clock to go out shooting rabbits.

Of course, I couldn't get out of it.

Bidge brought with him a large dog of no particular breed, a bit like a wolf-hound, though smaller than that. One of its flanks was almost bare of hair, and seemed to be formed of clustered pink nodules, a little like raw sweet-breads – some sort of growth I suppose. Luckily the animal kept well away from me and contented itself with emitting the occasional menacing growl in my direction. Bidge, in fact, bore a certain resemblance to his dog. He wore a saggy jacket with the collar turned up to show the basting, which made me feel cold, though it wasn't.

We set off in the direction of the mountain. Bidge nodded towards a side lane which led to a farmhouse, and said, "Got a bint up there, I have. Real juicy one. Only fourteen, she is." He asked me if I'd ever 'dipped my wick,' and I said not really. Actually I'm afraid I may have flushed. Anyhow I tried to change the subject by remarking that I'd never handled a gun before, and he asked when I was due to start my National Service. I said soon enough. He laughed and said gruffly, "They'll teach you a thing or two." So I said, "Yes, I expect they will. I expect I'll learn all about firearms." But he just laughed again and repeated, "They'll teach you a thing or two, and no mistake."

We turned up an inconspicuous, stone-walled path that was to lead onto the lower slopes of the mountain. Half way along it, the dog made a sudden swerve to the side and began scrabbling with its forepaws, then lunged forward to snap up something. A scaly tail flicked and twisted out of the side of its mouth. Some small rodent, obviously. Bidge yelled curses in Welsh, but the dog bounded away to a safe distance where it paused to jerk the thing back into its throat and polish it off in a few quick gulps. It seemed to have swallowed the creature whole, and I had a nauseating vision of it eventually expelling a hard, sharp-toothed skull through its anus.

We strode up the increasingly boulder-strewn gradient towards Garn Fawr, which seemed to get bigger and bigger without getting any closer as we approached it. It must be really huge. I was surprised to note that Bidge seemed to have less stamina for uphill walking than I did. Whether for that reason or not, he eventually stopped and said that this was a good place for rabbits. We took our position against a flat rock, and Bidge took the rifle out of its canvas sheath and showed me how to load the chamber and push it home with the bolt. He would take the first shot, to make sure we would have a rabbit stew tomorrow. I watched carefully, as I was determined not to disgrace myself when my turn came. We waited in silence for the bunnies to appear. The temperature had dropped, and I fancied that the breeze at our backs took its chill from the Buddha stones. Then Bidge grunted softly, took quick aim and fired. I hadn't even seen where the rabbit was until it leapt flappily up to drop out of sight behind a tussock. "I think I got it," Bidge said, and we went to look. He reached it first and held it up by its ears for my admiration. "There – right through the eye!" And sure enough, where the eye had been there was a ragged hole filling slowly with red ooze.

So we resumed our position, and I loaded the rifle successfully and waited again with my elbows on the hard stone. I was nervous of the moment when I would pull the trigger, as I was expecting a sharp recoil. People at Dad's depot have told me about sergeants grabbing the barrel of your rifle and thumping your shoulder with it and saying, "There – that's what to expect." I didn't realise that a .22 has no recoil to speak of. However, time passed and no more rabbits materialised, though Bidge did keep saying he could see them, but I couldn't. Eventually he said we'd just have to practise firing at pieces of paper, so he stuffed two – one for his target and one for mine – among the stiff grasses in the shelter between two rocks, and we took five shots each at them, which was all the ammunition he'd brought. The light was beginning to fail by now. But still, he hit his target all five times, and I didn't hit mine at all. We packed up and came home, saying little. Across the valley, the long ridge of a mountain lay like a log in a nearly-cold grate, the mists in front of it pale and fleecy, those beyond it like grubby smoke which once in a while parted to reveal fir trees outlined against a silver sky. Where the hump curved down at one end, the clouds were suffused with maroon and pink and yellow, the remnants of sunset. But I didn't think this was the sort of thing I could draw to Bidge's attention. I was almost shivering now. But he seemed no colder than he had been when we started out.

Of course I had to express gratitude, and emphasise how kind it had been of Bidge to go to so much trouble on my account, and, in Auntie Gwen's presence, generally make a joke of my own uselessness. Is it a joke? Can you ever quite be a joke to yourself – and if not, what can you be? I don't know when I've felt so unutterably miserable. I can't wait to get home.

III

High above the cove, he sits in a sheltered cleft of rock. Waves glimmering on the pure water seem strangely immobile – immobile as the surface of rippled glass. In the shadow of the fir-clad cliffs at the far side, the water is bottle green, sombre.

Perhaps a ship lies at anchor – rides at anchor. A Grecian vessel, say – a trireme. No, that won't do. Triremes were lean, stripped down, fighting ships – the equivalent of corvettes. Perhaps it could be Odysseus's ship, scarred and battered with long journeying, paint blistered and flaked... There is no-one to be seen. Below decks, the hammocks are empty.

Perhaps this is the island of Circe. Those sounds. The low moaning of pained cattle in distant byres. Bleatings and grunts oddly plaintive, as if straining towards the articulate – almost human.

Bear in mind the colours.

Clouds slate grey upon ash grey, rumpled as bedding, turbulent, unstill – and through them a shaft of silver light picks out the great cairn... Wasn't the Buddha transformed into a rock, or something? No, that's another idea altogether – to do with every stone partaking of the Buddha nature. Doesn't belong here. Did Ovid write about Circe?

Odysseus, hungry, seeking his lost oarsmen, spots a rabbit and silently sets an arrow to his great bow. A rabbit? I seem to remember rabbits were introduced from America in the 16th century, or something. Better make it a hare. He draws his great bow, aims, releases the arrow which, before the hare can react to the sound of its release, impales it through one eye to emerge, all blood-sticky, garnet-glittering, out of the other. And at once there is a terrible cry of agony, and as the hare writhes it grows and changes aspect, its ears retracting, its fore-legs clasping the rocks in desperation. Odysseus reaches his quarry with swift strides, but in that short time the hare has already transformed itself back into one of his shipmates.

Grey dead gorse still rooted in the fissures.

There's something called metamorphic rock. Must find out what that is.

Odysseus, weasel-witted, his skin salt-cured by the sea airs, crouches over the dead man in whose eye-sockets the now broken arrow is strangely lodged. He knows he is in the presence of forces against which even his wiles may prove unavailing. He turns up the collar of his tunic as if against a sudden, inexplicable chill. Unsure what to do next, he starts at the voice of distant thunder.

Sandals hung loosely from her belt by their leather thongs, blunt toes cuffing the buttercups, black ringlets braided with filaments of fine gold, she strides through the grass silently. Dark coils of hair under her armpits. Her sweat smells of crushed lemons. A mist follows her down the slope as if exhaled from the rocks behind her. Her lips twitch back in contempt or in anger – in what is almost a snarl.

Query: hadn't Odysseus left his great bow behind in Ithaca? Isn't there something about his wife's weedy suitors trying to draw it?

Her thighs. Her thighs are of the creamy cast of the patina of ancient marble. Her stride is restless, ruthless. The dogs that follow her – they are not hunting dogs – have intelligence in their eyes, but it is a subdued, almost defeated intelligence whose gaze is useless as one may imagine people's gaze in the dark of a tunnel. And beneath her, beneath her world, beneath all of them, flows the subterranean murmur of Homer's voice, a brook burbling over cobbles, a blind and buried stream. (Too self-conscious, perhaps?) Her chapel – her temple – is of stone grey-green and grey-yellow, tones reminiscent of the hand-tinted print or the hand-tinted postcard.

Odysseus experiences a stirring of the loins, and fears it because he cannot tell the reason for it. He sets off hurriedly back towards the shore.

Without warning the ship begins to rock, almost as if in a spasm, as a sudden squall scribbles its signature on the sea. The downpour releases every shade of grey as rain sheets this way and that, cross-hatching, suffused with pale colour of cloudbreak, of distant conifers, of other rainings across the island, of gorse yellow, of goat brown, of foxglove magenta in a sandy dell where...

Perhaps this could be done entirely with the colours – a symphony of infinitely mutable greys – forget the action altogether. A weather-drama with the people subsidiary? Stone and grass and water. And the sad, sad animals. Would that be possible?

Bone up on Ovid.

Letter to a Dog

ONE

Dear Doris,

I've just woken up. Haven't even made myself a coffee yet; and you'll remember how it conflicts with my nature to do anything at all before coffee. But no, I have just woken up, and straight away heaved on my old army greatcoat to sit down at my desk in obedience to an impulse – a whim, if you prefer – to communicate with you. I got up so abruptly that I'm still burdened with one of those dry, unsympathetic and useless morning erections: useless not simply because there's no-one to share it with, but because in any case it's of too impersonal a character to participate in any imaginable human activity. I mean, were I to be confronted with a woman this very instant, I should find it necessary, before proceeding further, to rid myself of this rude tool and equip myself with a fresh one customised, as it were, by the specific character of her appeal. I'm looking at the sky: a sober, rain-soaked Savile Row grey except for a narrow strip, almost at the horizon, where it frays away to expose a luminous turquoise which mutates subtly into the sort of tint you'd once have found in a woman's powder compact; and against this pastel strip are set the silhouettes of spires and cranes and towerblocks and skeletal gasometers.

So, you'll be wondering: do I disturb the dust of your terminal repose only to describe the sky to you? After all, your eyesight was never up to much even when you were young; and colour discriminations in the far distance were presumably outside the range of experiences for which evolution had fitted you. Yours was largely an olfactory world. Also auditory, of course... Yes, yes: already I see you shift your weight irritably from paw to paw as you would when being made to wait longer for a sliver of cheese from the grater than you thought reasonable. Very well, I'll tell you what brought you to mind. Just before I woke I was having one of those anthropological dreams I used to have quite often when I was looking into the subject, and this one was about a society where the human span was notionally subdivided into periods called 'doglives'. Each was of fifteen years, and each was given a name – Fido, Bonzo, Towser... I don't remember them all. Well, most dream ideas look pretty stupid once you're fully awake; but this one seemed to have something going for it. So, as the dream dissolved, I struggled to keep hold of the reasoning. Our first doglife, which brings us to the age of 15, is the time it takes us to become who we're going to be, if you see what I mean; and our second, to the age of 30, we spend acquiring the skills necessary to that being. From 30 to 45 we labour in the employment of those skills. The years from 45 to 60 are those in which our labour may be transmuted into wisdom; and our fifth and final doglife, up to the age of 75, is the one in which, if we're among the lucky for whom life's promise is fulfiled, all our accumulated experience may be returned to the world in the form of advice and example to our grandchildren. Neat, you'll agree. Of course, it was accepted that some people would live beyond the age of 75; but no new doglife was allocated for this – the extra years, which could in extreme cases be as many as 30, being seen as some sort of a limbo in which people simply spiral down into endless and ever more tedious self-repetition. So it's a scheme that matches our own culture fairly snugly. But I wonder what a dog would make of it.

The strip under the dark bolt of the clouds is now a shiny graphite on which London is limned in silver. Here and there a window finds the pale sun and flashes an inscrutable message at us. At us? At me.

As often happens, I know where the dream came from. Yesterday I was thinking about Stonehenge, wondering what sort of people they were who built it. You'll have seen the image from encyclopaedias, hairy men in hairy loin-cloths brandishing clubs... Then I thought: suppose Stonehenge was built around 1500 BC, that's to say 3,500 years ago; then at the standard estimate of 25 years to a generation, we're separated from those people by about 140 generations. A hundred and forty ancestors isn't very many if you imagine them all together – at a birthday party, say, or in a fairly empty cinema. What's more, the 'generation' is a bit of a misleading concept. If you think of whole three-score-and-ten life-spans end to end, you're down to 50. And I have to add, too, that the way time speeds up as one nears one's final doglife makes the stone age seem closer than ever – a mere stone's-throw away. Of course, all this is nothing we didn't know, really. The people who built Stonehenge could have used a computer if you'd shown them how. Doubtless they were prey to superstition; but then I read recently that 90 percent of Americans, even today, still believe in God...

The erection, I notice, has lapsed: that primal, tribal pole whose impersonality is enhanced by the witness it bears to my shortcoming: for I differ in one important respect from every one of my ancestors, the many hundreds, many thousands of them reaching far back beyond the neolithic, the palaeolithic, whose callused hands knocked flints together and groomed each other's ginger pelts on the shores of lakes long evaporated: that I, alone among that expectant horde, have failed to reproduce, have writ finis to our line, have broken their faith and squandered their immemorial efforts. You at least have not such a thing on your conscience. But you see now, I dare say, that the skies are not without relevance. In a few brief minutes, the world can alter its complexion twice. Two lifetimes could have passed – dog or human making no difference. So trust me.

I draw my khaki coat around me, my ginger coat, and remember polishing the brass buttons against a brass slide that stopped the Brasso staining the fabric – if you were clever at it. But I'm telling a little white lie here, aren't I? I didn't bring my coat with me out of the army. This is one I bought in the sixties, when military gear was fashionable among the hippie young. I bought it so as to enjoy the feeling of never having to polish those buttons ever again.

Palaeolithic, Holocene, Pleistocene, Pliocene... pretty names, aren't they, that we've given to our far past? *The Children's Argosy of Knowledge.* And such delicate drawings of mammoth and mastodon scattering the puny hunters pell-mell. As a child I never spotted the underlying contradiction between style and content. Children are nature's realists – or perhaps I mean 'positivists'. Yet still I try to visualise that ginger-pelted forebear whilst knowing I have no valid visual idiom in which to do so. No valid verbal idiom, come to that. *Want meat. Mammoth soon. Axe blunt as old Harry.* Crude stereotyping of the primitive? Well, all right; but there must have been a point, somewhere along the line, when complex articulation hadn't yet evolved or been invented – whichever. I remember once watching a three-year-old maddened with frustration at finding himself unable to say what he wanted to say because he didn't have the words for it. The potential meaning was so palpably there, unable to deliver. Did my forebear, likewise, know there were things he wanted to say but couldn't – and resent it? Did you too? So often people remark, of an animal, "Look, she's trying to say..." or, "If only she could speak, she'd be telling us..." It's a strange thought: that there should be ideas which can't be articulated, yet which enjoy some spectral, potential existence regardless. Perhaps that's why I choose you as recipient for my confidences.

Besides, who else would give me the time of day now?

It's clear, though – questions of the inexpressible aside – that things can be said to a dog which one could never bring oneself to say to a fellow human. It has to do with the nature of the intimacy which bound us. For one thing, there's no human being, however close, of whom it can be said that I've shovelled up and disposed of their excreta for years on end, or that I have watched with idle curiosity as they experienced intercourse. Nor would I wish it otherwise.

My cuffs are fraying. I look at my buttons: tarnished, unloved. Want coffee. Dress soon. My mind harks back to National Service, and to the time a handful of us cycled from the camp at Pewsey to visit West Kennet long barrow. I dare say nowadays it's surrounded by a razor-wire fence with video surveillance and portaloos and a franchised hamburger outlet; but in those days you just took a muddy path up the side of a field and there it was, and you walked straight in. A fair old piece of dry-stone walling, we thought. Traditional craft, no less. Handed down. Impressive example. But I remember being somehow disappointed. I'd been expecting atmosphere – you know, ghosts – and instead it was simply there, minding its own business. Maybe they'd cemented the floor to protect it, I'm not sure. But at all events, there was no sign of the ancestors. It was only later, at night, in bed in the Nissen hut where the groaning, snuffling, somnolent forms of my comrades somehow found resonance with serried niches of the emptied ossuary, that the strangeness came home to me: not the strangeness of 'atmosphere' as such, but the strangeness of the behaviour of people engaged in such commonplace activity as dry-stone walling, yet on such a demanding scale and to such rare purpose: a purpose, though, which for something like a millennium seemed perfectly comprehensible and normal to people who, if you'd shown them how to use a computer... But of course we didn't have computers ourselves in those distant days. Not a glimmer, except in some boffins' madcap fantasies. And as for comrades – well, it depends what you mean – as old Joad would have said – by 'comrade'. It wasn't so long since these companions in tribulation had, while I slept, carefully placed my dangling hand in a bucket of water so that I pissed the bed. Oh yes, it works – take my word for it. Snap inspection; reek of stale ammonia: "Put that man on a charge!" So much for *Kameradschaft*. So much for that mutinous battleship. You're not supposed to mind. Meanwhile, my ginger-back forebear lies face down on the lake-shore, blood curling lazily into the lapping ripples, skull smashed with blunt rocks. What has happened, then? Last time we met him he was gormlessly clonking flints together. Hang around – I'll think of something.

I really am going to break off for a coffee now. It's getting Uncle Willie in here. Talking of willies, though, I wish I hadn't been so hard on that hard-on. They don't occur so regularly these days, and perhaps it's unwise to discourage them when they do. Still, I'm not really complaining. It's better than in your teens, when you could-n't even stand next to a woman in a crowded bus without risk of indecent exposure. Did my forebear have a mate, I wonder? Well of course he did, by definition: by the bare fact of being defined as my forebear. How enviable to have a mate by definition!

Right, then: here I am: coffee'd, dressed, warmed and feeling a bit more human. Sorry, old mutt – no offence meant. I'll tell you what I was thinking about while the coffee was brewing, just to show you what daft things we humans waste our computational power on. I was wonder-ing whether there actually was a time, ever, when the capacity for speech was fully present in our brains but language hadn't yet been invented. I mean, did language and the brain evolve in tandem, step by microscopic step, one gene for nouns, another for prepositions and then – a few thousand years later – another for subordinate clauses; or was that hard-wired grammar they talk about the once-and-once-only mutational gift of our common African Mum? It's not out of the question. It's not unknown for species to be endowed with capacities its members know nothing about. That chap Haldane – the communist – once asked what evolutionary advantage a sea-lion gained from being able to balance a ball on the end of its nose. Well, doubtless there are two views on this. As my actual Mum used to say, there are two sides to every question. But frankly: what is the point in my mulling over such a matter, while the coffee brews, when people far better qualified than myself have already addressed it, probably without success? Can I help them resolve the conundrum? No. I'd be better occupied foraging for groceries, looking for a mate, getting my skull smashed in... But there we have it. If I'm to work out what may have happened to young ginger-back, I have, perforce, to address such questions as whether, for him and his tribe, language was immanent or merely imminent. That's a distinction we were taught at school. So even for us, you see, language doesn't come entirely naturally – though I suspect my penchant for pedantry owes less to English lessons than to having lived my life accurate to the penny.

School. Now there's something you never had to endure, eh? In fact, when I think of all the things you never had to endure, I feel all afresh the injustice of those glances of long-suffering, put-upon, Job-like fortitude you used to cast at us from under the table, head laid wearily on your outstretched paws... But this is no time for recriminations. Let by-gones be by-gones. In any case, no great harm came of it. Still, I'll tell you a story about school, because you may be interested. As you may know, school is an institution wherein the fundamental corpus of human knowledge – that without which we may scarcely even be defined as human – is supposed to be passed from generation to generation, world without end. And is it? Well, certainly I learned the difference between 'immanent' and 'imminent', and one or two other such things which I might equally have picked up in the course of general experience. But I did, in addition, learn one very important lesson; though whether the school's founders and donors and all those majestically extinct families immortalised on its escutcheon would have considered this one of the defining elements of species knowledge I'm in no position to say. It happened like this. Behind our school buildings were the playing fields; and it was permitted for us to walk around these fields during our lunch breaks. But it was not permitted for us to stray from the path onto the grass. Well, that was reasonable enough. The staff didn't want their carefully tended turf to be progressively scuffed and trampled. One day, however, as I was strolling round the field during a lunch break, I found myself confronted by three prefects coming the other way. Prefects? Yes. They are the equivalents of NCOs in the army or Kapos in a Lager: people given limited authority over their fellows as a means of splitting the loyalties of the underlings. This particular form derives from the so-called public school system; and my own school was one particularly keen to ape its betters by making the most of its tatty antiquity: a world of blazers blazoned with nothing to write home about. Nevertheless, those grim and grimy ancestral relics did serve the purpose of attracting some suitably toffee-nosed kids, who in their turn helped sustain the place in its own self-estimation... Anyway, as I say, I was approached by these three prefects who, walking abreast on the narrow path, left me no room to avoid them; and I thus had no choice but, as politely as possible, as unobtrusively, hoping to slip unnoticed beneath the lofty threshold of their scorn, to step onto the grass – just one step, you understand, executed with one foot only – in order to allow them to pass. Immediately I was told that I had committed a serious infraction of regulations and must report on Saturday morning to receive six strokes of the cane. Well, it so happened that our school, being an institution not uncontaminated by liberalism, had an appeals procedure for the benefit of those who considered they'd been unjustly treated. Feeling that my treatment was unjust by any normal standards, I applied for a hearing by the tribunal. The tribunal consisted of three prefects, two of whom – yes, I'm sure you've guessed it – two of whom, including the president, were among the three who had imposed the punishment in the first place. That taught me a lesson I've never forgotten: a lesson about how authority works. You weren't supposed to mind. That was what was so galling. But I did mind; and I continued to mind – continued for years, fantasising revenge.

Eventually I stumbled across what seemed to me a method tailor-made for my requirements. A young man whom I met at night-school when I was studying accountancy for the City and Guilds, and with whom I used to walk part of the way home, had an alarming habit. He would choose a moment when a heavy lorry or bus was moving swiftly up to overtake us, then say, "Cross now." Luckily I was always too prickly a character to take orders mechanically, otherwise I might not have survived this friendship. I've often wondered what would have happened if, in a moment of preoccupation, I had actually stepped off the kerb at his prompting. People following behind would, of course, have testified that I wasn't pushed. "He just walked in front of it – just like that! Can't imagine what came over him..." And I wondered, too, whether my friend – well, acquaintance – seriously desired this outcome. Ever gullible, I tended to assume not. But some years later I heard that he'd abandoned his job with a reputable firm in order to act as personal consultant to... well, no names no pack-drill, but let's just say to someone whose generous donations to charity were frequently reported in the press. I suppose it was the idea of stepping from a track designated safe that made the connection seem so apt. Needless to say, I never saw any of those prefects again; but my mind was slowly calmed by the thought that, should I ever spot one of them walking along a busy street, I would unhesitatingly draw up alongside him and, at the approach of the first heavy vehicle, issue the order: "Cross now!"

I realise this story may appear a little outré to you. You were never caned in your life, were you, Doris? The idea of beating a dog with a stick was repugnant to us, let alone the idea of fixing a date for it and performing the act in a room used for no other purpose, a room furnished only with a glass-fronted cupboard full of birches and, bizarrely, in the middle of the floor, a fully plumbed bath – brown-stained, caked with scaly matter – over which we were obliged to lean, our pants around our ankles... It would have seemed bestial – if that is quite the word.

So. The ginger-back, panting heavily, sweat matting his fur, arrives at a point where the river debouches into the lake. Perhaps we should give him a name. Let's call him Ggarax. Tired, using his knuckles to expedite his progress, Ggarax turns left with the intention of continuing along the lakeshore where the going is easier; but there, barring his progress, baring his huge teeth, is the big grey-back – Bborog. As his pursuers swarm over the boulders towards him, Ggarax hears a cry. It is his mate, away in the house of isolation, who must surely, he thinks, be giving birth this very moment. Only when the placenta has been eaten by wart-hogs will the tribe again recognise her existence and make their way to the lonehouse chanting, "New person now. New person now." And that will be too late to divert his enemies from their present purpose. Had these people, I wonder, made the causal connection in their minds between sex and childbirth? Probably so. I would imagine it to have been one of the first insights vouchsafed by the gift of naming, which is the gift of generalisation releasing us from the prison of the particular – right? – first step, that is, on the long road to nanotechnology and DNA sequencing. Yes, then, Ggarax knows it is his own child who is being born at the very moment when the young males catch up with him, drag him down and, hoping to ingratiate themselves with Bborog who, knowing his rival is already defeated, is indifferent to his fate and plays no further part in it, smash at his head with stones until his brains leak into the wind-chopped shallows...

"Hup! two-three-four; hup! two-three-four... At the double!" Full kit. Sweating like a pig. The two red-caps sitting with their feet up – on purpose – they'd never normally be seen slouching like that... "Getting a bit tired, are we? Getting nowhere fast, are we? Well, we all feel like that at times, don't we, George? Tell you what: we'll be generous: let you relax with a few press-ups – say fifty for starters. That all right? I said, *That all right*? Answer when you're spoken to, or we'll start taking our jobs a bit more seriously – won't we, George? Had your type in here before, you know – those that look down on us, don't think we're worth a civil word... eh, George?"

One day, when I was stationed in Cyprus – evening, it was – we were on our way back from a patrol, and I saw this shepherd bringing his goats home. There was a dry-stone-walled enclosure with a low stone shed or sty in it; and from inside the sty came an absolute bedlam of high-pitched bleating: it was the kids, I realised, waiting for their milk. So the shepherd went into the enclosure and opened up the sty, and the sound became deafening as the kids all rushed out for their mothers; but they didn't bother going round to the gap in the wall, no, they just spilled straight over it in a sort of cappuccino foam like a freak wave breaking over the sea wall onto a promenade. It's something I've never forgotten. So that's how I see the hairy men foaming over the rocks as they close in on Ggarax. He turns towards the lake. The horizon seems to beckon him with all the metaphysical power of a latent aspiration; and although no human being has ever swum, has ever tried to do so, he summons up the image of animals dog-paddling and in desperation launches himself into the deeper water between the rocks, only to find himself gasping helplessly for breath and thrashing backwards to where his feet can touch bottom, struggling to get the wet fur out of his eyes; and it is while he is so engaged that the first stone strikes his skull with a sound like an earthenware pot cracking... But no, they wouldn't have had pots, not in those days – like an ostrich egg cracking, or a gourd, or... But again, that's only when they're empty. Perhaps I'm barking up the wrong tree with the sound. So much to think about, isn't there? And anyway, it's a moot point whether you can formulate a simile if you haven't got a developed language. I don't see any real reason why not, though. The image of those goats, looking like a wave of foam, doesn't need a word to link it – just the recollection of the similar movement. Perhaps so long as the potential of language is there... In fact perhaps that's just what the potential of language is. But I've seen it said, more times than once, that children who grow up among animals – feral children – that they'll never learn to speak at all if they haven't learnt by the time they're nine or ten. The capacity shrivels up. So you can imagine the human race going for generations with the brain-circuitry for speech fully evolved, but no-one having anyone to learn it from, because there isn't any yet.

And then music: what about music? There are people who can play all manner of highbrow stuff by the age of four, and seem pre-programmed just for that sort of a life; yet really complicated music didn't exist until – I don't know – say a thousand years ago. So evolution hardly comes into it. Suppose there'd been one of those musical prodigy types: how would that have revealed itself back in the stone age? D'you remember that horse they had on television that was supposed to be able to distinguish between different composers? During your time, I think it was: horse called Plurabelle...

Well, now. Let's say they've had swan for supper – a swan caught with great difficulty with the aid of woven fronds. What they actually did was to tangle its fearsome wings and then drown it by holding it under for a long time – a job requiring six men – while its long neck flexed like a hose as it struggled for air. The swan has been cut up crudely into hunks and charred in somewhat hit-and-miss fashion on the hot stones of the fire. The choicest cuts have been allocated to Bborog, as is only proper. Bones have been split for their marrow – I assume swan bones must have marrow – and the offal flung beyond the notional boundary of the encampment to where the dogs lurk, padding back and forth, waiting, always waiting. The presence of the dogs is a source of mild but constant anxiety. They have been known, when famished, to snatch a baby; and therefore, if they come too close, they'll be pelted with stones until they retreat again to the tacitly agreed distance. Yet they are never driven completely away, partly because they would in any case always come back, and partly because they can be relied upon to detect the approach of predators long before a person would, and to alert the camp by barking. So, if their presence is to be tolerated, there is no option but to feed them.

The feathers of the swan, too, are the property of Bborog, and are scattered to supplement the leaves on which he sleeps. The drifts of snowy white among the green and the amber are agreeable to the eye, as is their softness to Bborog's aging muscles. The sight of his great flawed and craggy head at rest upon such a resplendent cushion stirs a nameless impulse of respect, partakes of a quality that would now be called 'regal'.

Some days later, a young female – Kkinthe might be her name – detects a delicate sound, something between a warble and a moan, among the windswept grasses. It is a sound she does not recognise. Squatting cautiously, she parts the grasses expecting to find some juicy insect or the nest of some ground-dwelling bird. What she sees is a white thing. It's a bone: a broken-off and sun-dried end of the swan's thigh bone which the ants have hollowed and which makes this sound as the wind gusts across it. Kkinthe picks it up. The sound stops. She holds it at various angles to the wind, but cannot recapture the effect that was achieved by chance. Perhaps it was not the effect of the wind after all. Perhaps there is something bad about the bone, something to be afraid of. But the sound was so gentle and companionable. She blows at the bone. Nothing. Again nothing. And then, by fluke, she blows at the right angle. The sound comes back. It is she who has made it, she is sure. She keeps trying, and eventually finds the way to make the sound happen every time. It is just a matter of how you angle your lips to the place where it is broken. She is delighted by the sound, and pokes the bone into her hair for safe keeping.

When she has time, Kkinthe looks for more bones. She

is young, unmated, and still has something of a child's curiosity; and she wants to give this good-sounding thing to her friend, but does not want to give her hers. So she looks for more bones. Eventually she finds one, but it is hollow both ends, and makes no sound however hard she tries blowing. Then she thinks of putting her thumb over the hole at one end. It makes a sound. But what amazes her now is that the sound is not the same as the one the first bone makes. She makes the two sounds, one after the other, over and over. It is like a bird's call; but it is *her* call – *her* two notes; and the two notes seem to belong together, to want to live together. Eventually Bborog becomes annoyed by these two notes. He looms up behind Kkinthe, snatches the bones from her and throws them far away into the bushes, and he hits her hard. Ggarax has seen this happen; and the next time he returns with a trout, having given the mandatory half to Bborog, he gives the remainder to Kkinthe.

OK so far? How about the bit about the dogs – did that ring true? Well, there must have been a stage when it was something like that. After all, other apes don't keep dogs. Then, from that point on, it would have begun to have positive survival value for a dog to be trustworthy rather than to have your baby for dinner while your back was turned. Ergo... But one thing I haven't paid attention to is the question of sexual organisation within the group. Is it still a question of the dominant male with his harem, and younger males being kicked out to fend for themselves once they reach maturity; or are we into quasi-stable pair-bonding, nuclear families ganging together for mutual protection like today's hunter-gatherers? However quickly mutations are now thought to happen – and what do palaentologists mean by 'quickly', anyway? – the change can't have taken place over-night. There must have been a period, whether centuries or millennia, when the norms were, as people say these days, contested. That's my theory. "Oh yes, old Pisser's got a theory about everything – haven't you, Pisser?" "Hey, Pisser – got a theory about the action of the human waterworks, then?" And they all turn and laugh – all the hut, in various stages of kitting up, they all turn and laugh at me. All those faces. Once it's settled that you're to be the butt of all jokes, there's no appeal, no sympathy. "How was jankers? Bring you your tea in bed, did they?" "Didn't even send us a postcard, he didn't!" Friendship counts for nothing. You could win the Nobel prize for speculative palaeontology and they'd jeer at you for it.

A silence descends, and all faces turn upon Ggarax. Bborog gives vent to a great booming roar, then bares his teeth – his canines, if you'll allow the allusion. Ggarax does not bare his teeth; but he stands his ground; and he makes eye-contact. That is not done. No-one does it. The troop are watching, their fur prickling with anticipation. Bborog roars again. Ggarax grips Kkinthe by her shoulder and turns, guiding her, to move away. Bborog seems nonplussed. Ggarax has made no gesture of submission; but then he has made no gesture of aggression either. He has backed off, true; but at the same time he has taken Kkinthe with him. Bborog must either give chase, which might seem a faintly undignified reaction, or pretend that no matter of any substance has been at issue. By moving away, Ggarax has repudiated any challenge to his authority as Leader; and what is one female more or less to someone of his seniority? Slowly, as if shrugging off some minor irritant, Bborog turns and shambles back to his bed-heap. But he will not forget.

And me – washed up, unshaven, spent as Onan's seed?

Want Kkinthe. Like softness of fur. Like sounds she makes with bones.

TWO

The sky is the colour of an old dish-rag – even to the marginal decorative blue stitching, befouled as the rest of it. Rain splatters occasionally against the window. Somewhere under my ribs a flint spear-tip lodges, heavy yet razor-edged. On the roof opposite, a hunched and trembling pigeon receives fussy attentions from two or three others who take turns to try and interest him in activity, in flying: a summoning of small sympathies: the most that can be hoped for. And in my case, more.

Some mornings I hesitate for long minutes before easing myself out of bed. I feel as if my insides are populated. Yes, I know that's an odd word to use, but it's the closest I can get to describing it, because it's not pain exactly, just a sense that things are not as they should be and have always been; and I'm afraid that if I rise too quickly... well, I don't know exactly what I'm afraid of, either. But for all that, I know a commitment when I see one; and I know I have to continue what I began: this explanation, this self-exculpation if you will; let's just call it this letter. That way no-one need take premature umbrage.

You, I'm sure, would be the first to note the fatuity of my yesterday's day-dream: a meeting of true minds in the stamping grounds of the primaeval rhinoceros. Mills and Boon might welcome it as a fresh angle; but it's emphatically not what life's about. I mean, is it what your life was about? My punishment was to be haunted last night by the memory of Sergeant Rudekamp: nemesis; one of many. Actually it's not so many years since I ran into him. We went for a drink together for old times' sake – no hard feelings, and all that codswallop – and he took the opportunity to lay bare his philosophy for my benefit:

"Remember that slag used to swab out the Naafi at

Limassol – Oddjobs, we used to call her, and for good reason. Seen a good few of her sort, I can tell you; but wow! And she was anybody's – anybody's. Except yours, perhaps – eh? So why did you have to come on so prissy with her? That's what I never understood. You could have made her feel trash – absolute trash – and you'd have got whatever you wanted. So why not? I'll tell you why not. It's 'cause you're weak. You're afraid to hurt someone 'cause you think you might need them one day. But what could you have needed from her? In any case, you got it wrong. The more you trash them the more they come back. Or if not, find another. But you – you never understood the simplest thing that I learned in my first class at school: there's always got to be someone at the bottom of the heap. What does a teacher do? She's got a new class of rebellious kids in front of her, and she knows it's her or them, and the clock's started counting already and if she can't establish control very quickly she'll be at their mercy for the rest of the year; so what does she do? She finds the one she can ridicule – that's what she does if she knows her onions – because she knows then she can get all the others on her side laughing at that one poor bleeder. So from the moment she enters that classroom she's alert as a hunting dog, watching: and what she's watching for is a sign of weakness in somebody, something she can lock on to, something she can work on, something she can mock in the crude sort of way that won't go over the others' heads too much, because then it would be no help to her. My first year in school, it was me: I was the sacrificial goat. I had a bit of a twitch, a nervous tic; and this teacher, she spotted it within minutes; and from then on, whenever the class threatened to get disruptive, it would be, 'Young Rudekamp seems to be winking at us over there. What is it, Rudekamp? Are you hoping to estab-lish some sort of a mutually caring relationship?' And at that, the class would laugh uproariously, even though they hadn't the foggiest what 'mutually' meant. And so the heat was off her; she'd got control again. But don't go thinking I resent it. Next year I made bloody sure it wasn't going to be me – got a hold on my nerves by sheer effort of will power – but like I say I don't resent it, looking back, no, because I can see that the misery of one child is a small price to pay for a quiet classroom where all the others can learn except the one who's shitting himself; and of course, the more that one doesn't learn, the more teacher has got a grip over him, hasn't she? So there you are. It's how life works, my friend. That's the secret of relationships in all spheres, this man doesn't love his wife, that one loves her too much. Go for it: be alert for the weakness, and then go for it. But you – you let resentment cloud your sense. You resent the facts of life. So you never had the pleasure of the facts of life with Oddjobs. And I don't suppose you ever grasped why those men played that trick on you with the bucket of water, eh? They knew, you see. They'd noticed how you always took a precautionary leak before parade. They knew that was your weakness. Here, let me buy you another pint."

Dreams can be instructive if you look at them the right way. The fact that I dreamt about Rudekamp last night – he was standing in front of me pissing into a bucket, and the others were all grinning, and I was frightened of what he might be intending to do with it when he'd filled it – well, the fact that I dreamt about him meant I recognised that what was wrong with my little stone-age narrative wasn't just the soppy stuff. The real wishful thinking lay in the idea that personality could out-face power. And yet I'm not quite sure. Certainly that's how Rudekamp would see it – not a doubt about that. But somehow, once in a while, by some fluke of circumstances in which it really might undermine a leader's authority for him to be seen exercising it trivially, perhaps... I don't know. Would Bborog really have attacked me – I mean attacked Ggarax – physically, when the conditions of challenge had not been met? The trick is to present him with stimuli which sidestep or confuse his instinctual responses. How about Rudekamp, then? He, I imagine, would respond in such a situation with subtle and not-so-subtle imputations of effeminacy: 'lady's man'; 'lounge lizard'... But Bborog wouldn't have been up to that. Besides, the task I'd set myself was to pinpoint a moment in the change from polygamy to monogamy – a change broadly recognised, even if certain *droits de seigneur* do continue to be claimed right through into our own times. It's like those things we amaze ourselves with as children: that there must have been one person who was the first, the very first ever, to light a fire on purpose; just as there must have been one ancestral dog who was the first to risk licking a human's hand. Would you have been so brave? And do you, on balance, regret it?

It would be ungracious of me not to mention, while we're on this subject, that a dog can lend bravery to a man. Do you recall, I wonder, that occasion when you and I were taking a stroll through some woodland and came to a large flat clearing where a cricket match was in progress? With a clonk of wood on willow – 'wielding the willow' – that used to be the popular phrase – the ball came streaking towards us. A fielder in immaculate white sprinted to intercept it; but you got there first, snapped up the ball and went running with it in teasing circles around the man while all the distant brawnies yelled abuse at us both. I eventually managed to get you to sit, took the ball from you and tossed it – now tooth-scarred and slicked with a biosphere of canine saliva – to the fielder, who was I think a little wobbly from turning in tight circles to try and grab you, because he came at a slight stagger as I clipped you to the lead, obviously intending to give us a piece of his mind. Before he could find words adequate to his fury, and before I could censor my own, I said very mildly, "Sorry, mate – she thinks it's a game." That took a moment to sink in; then he became almost apoplectic. He lunged towards me as if meaning to clout me. But he saw the sudden curl of your lip, and noted the low growl from deep in your belly, and had the sense to back off. I continued my walk at an almost exaggerated saunter, enjoying our little triumph; though I have to admit I was relieved when I found myself back among the trees.

Perhaps – now here's a thought! – perhaps it was the company of dogs that ushered in monogamy by making it more hazardous for the leader to enforce his universal conjugal demands. But it's a flimsy theory. The first we see of dogs is in those paintings on cave walls; and there it seems more a question of canine pack helping human pack than of any individual loyalties – though who's to know? I look at those murals and I hear the shouts, the shouts of men giving instructions to the dogs: "Sweep round to the left!" – "A bit to the right!" – "OK, now drive the elk this way..." Obviously there'd have been language by that time – too much diversity of objects to handle without – even if it was a very cumbersome language, all verbs irregular, plurals formed any-old-how. Or maybe they'd already got past that stage. Somebody, as I keep on saying, must have thought all this through. Perhaps if I were to read books about it I'd learn something. I did try once upon a time – reading proper science books, that is. But it was too much of a slog: all that detail, the broad picture getting lost in a mush of qualifications. Much better to read the occasional column in a newspaper, or wait and watch a TV programme when they've sorted their ideas out.

Let me tell you something on the subject of education – because it's interesting the things that affect you in life. I never made much headway with the lingo in Cyprus. Never tried, to be quite honest; put off for a start by the different alphabet, though I did get to be able to recognise place-names eventually just from the look of them. But people treat you better if you're polite to them; so I'd taught myself to say 'ef-charisto' – which means 'thank you'. Then one day the padre happened to hear me saying that to someone; and he went out of his way to give me a little lecture to the effect that it's basically the same word as 'Eucharist' – as in church – and that the Spanish for that is 'mercedes', which in German is a make of car. He leaned back with a smile of professional benevolence. I realised many years later that he'd probably been trying to make some sort of a point about the interpenetration of the secular and the divine, and had been waiting to see whether I cottoned on. But at the time I took something quite different from it – I was only nineteen, after all – something like a realisation that you can follow words wherever they lead you, and the thoughts will tag along too. It was back to things like 'imminent' and 'immanent', which I'd shrugged off with all the rest of the pompous guff of schooldays as thankfully as I'd chucked my monogrammed cap onto the bonfire in the park on my way home. But it stuck this time.

Dogs, for example, and the names we give you. You, my exquisite Doris! Some people call their dogs things like Prince or Sultan; but those are a particular sort of people who want the animal to stand in for some quality they lack. There was a kid at primary school once told me he wanted a dog; and when I asked what for, he said, "To bite people with." But you didn't need a name like Prince to protect me against the crazed cricketer, did you? Most people call dogs something a trifle silly. Even the generic words – mutt, pooch, schnauzer – not to mention commonplace nick-names such as muddlegump or nettle-rash... Is it that we find dogs inherently absurd; or are we trying to draw a cloak of jocularity over something we prefer not to confront, to set you as a character in a comedy where all that may be done to you will take on the quality of the jolly, the rib-tickling? It's a thought with the properties of a pain. I don't think I'm ready to face up to it.

Meanwhile I gaze at the grey world out of a streaked window and try to imagine Kkinthe's soft fur, soft as the fur on a dog's tummy, my face buried in it for comfort, feeling her breathing, hearing her soft grunts as she caresses my head and lazily squeezes my lice between thumb and forefinger... Never have got any of that from Marge, would I? It'd have been a case of, "Get on with it, then, or else let me have some sleep. I've done a hard day's work, even if you haven't." Still, we all have a right to a drop of fantasy, don't we? What would life be without it? And it takes my mind away from worries about the future: how a District Nurse would get up to me here, for example, when the other tenants insist the downstairs door has to be kept locked at all times because it's so easy to break in. You have to think ahead. But I'll always avoid it for as long as humanly possible.

Once when I was courting Marge – talk about pre-history! – and we were having a meal at a little *ristorante* we thought of as 'ours', a chap called Fred Talcott came in whom I hadn't seen since I was demobbed. So I waved him over to join us. When eventually Marge went to powder her nose – which was what women did in those days instead of peeing – I asked him what he thought of my new bird; and he said, "Sorry, matey, but I find her culpably la-di-dah." That's the sort of phrase he was inclined to come out with. In fact I think it was his example, rather than anything the padre said, that was responsible for stretching my taste in reading-matter beyond the green paper-backs with the murderous crosses: 'If You're Nervy, Don't Read Hervey'. And that's something that has helped keep me on an even keel in these long days of solitary idleness.

You never knew this place, of course. You'd be saddened to see me now – especially if you thought this was a situation you were going to have to share. I'll tell you how it came about. Once I'd finished my National Service, I did what everyone did in those days: took a menial job to keep the wolf from the door while I slaved my guts out at night-school to get the qualifications for something better. Since I'd decided on a career in accountancy, I found work as an office boy – do they still have office boys, I wonder? – in the wages department of a retail chain. I worked with a will. I equipped myself with a presentable handwriting by prac-tising the 'Italian' style which had recently come into vogue, and which is still occasionally to be seen – you can date people by it to within a few years. I learned to operate the telephone exchange, with its morbid numbered eyeballs that dropped down like the upturned eyes of drowned men. I could ink the drum of a Gestetner to perfection. I even became quite a spiv on the comptometer – though such monotonous tasks were usually given to girls, who were assumed to have no mental processes of their own to get in the way of them. Above all, of course, I learned to make the tea to everybody's satisfaction. None of these talents, I should explain to you, has been required in an office for donkey's years. Even the tea is now dispensed by machine – usually to nobody's satisfaction.

So anyhow, I got my diploma; wage increase; promo-tion; strategic move sideways... It took a year or two; but eventually I landed myself a job with Feal & Divot; and I looked set for life. And I did all the things one does. I got the house and the mortgage, and the wife, and I moved up the property ladder to a better house, a semi with a garden backing onto the golflinks; and the garden had a *get your 'air cut!* lawn and azaleas and a pool that was big enough to sit beside – so you could say things like, "I think I'll take my apéritif beside the pool" – though you couldn't have swum more than two strokes in it, and nude cement goddesses in lieu of gnomes. And I learned to drive, and I bought a BMW. Pisser – a BMW! Rudekamp should have seen me in those days. But I'd forgotten him. I'd forgotten it all – the three prefects, the jocular MPs, all of it – or at least, I never gave a thought to such matters, which may or may not be the same thing. I guess I'd forgotten West Kennet, too.

Marge wanted kids, naturally; and so did I – or at least I persuaded myself that kids were the right thing to want. But, in the event, it was Not To Be. So we settled for letting you have a litter before you were spayed, as it's supposed to be psychologically beneficial to a bitch, stops her getting over-weight later in life and so forth. Not that you were allowed to keep them for more than a few weeks. That's not what dogs want, the experts opine. I still remember one of them, the youngest to survive, a little tiddle we used to call 'fruit bat' because its face was all scrunched up – though here we were in error, as I later discovered on a visit to the reference library, since fruit bats turn out always to have foxy profiles. Even pleasantries have to be researched, it seems. Never mind...

All this carried on for more than a doglife – yours, in fact – my third – and I really did think it was going to continue like that for ever, though I'm not sure what I thought the point was. But then the day came when I was called up to those realms where the carpets are thicker and the paintings browner, and the doors close more quietly, and was told in no uncertain terms that I had – and I quote – "displayed excessive zeal" in my promotion of the client's interests. Well, I'd assumed that was what was expected of me; and I still believe it was. One of my Mum's sayings was, "A nod's as good as a wink to a blind horse." I could never work out quite what that meant; but I'm sure this was a circumstance in which she'd have said it. I didn't, though. I think what had really happened was that the Revenue had, with a certain over-zealousness of their own, decided to look in unaccustomed detail at some of our audits; and mine either had, by sheer fluke, been the ones which caught their eye, or had been more spectacular in their stretching of the imagination than some of the others, or else the upper echelons had decided to use me as a sort of lightning conductor by diverting the inspectors' attentions in my direction – "Have to say, to be quite honest with you, we've been beginning to have our own suspicions about this chap; but you know how it is – can't check up on every detail of every employee's work, have to take something on trust..." I received a handshake that was silver rather than golden, but was clearly meant as a buy-off. The precise words were, "We now consider this matter closed – is that understood?" "Yes, sir," I said. I actually called the bastard 'sir' while he was sacking me. But they could easily have stopped the cheque, couldn't they? And that's when I remembered the three prefects.

I took a lengthy holiday in the sun, partly to make up to Marge, partly to lend credence to the line I intended to take when seeking fresh employment: that I'd wanted to re-energise myself for fresh challenges now that I felt myself to be at the peak of my capabilities. But the glowing testimonial I'd brought away from Feal & Divot seemed oddly unhelpful when appended to job applications; and I began to wonder whether, when approached for amplification, they weren't taking the opportunity to hedge it with dark hints – "Can't be faulted on his expertise. Depends what sort of a character you're looking for, I suppose. No, I'd just as soon you didn't ask us to say anything further..." Whatever the truth, I was left in little doubt that I was on the scrap heap. So that was that. First the car had to go. Then Marge went. We sold up the big house, and I took out a mortgage on this place with my share – which still left me sufficient in reserve so long as there were no more holidays. I've generally been able to supplement my funds with a bit of hole-and-corner business consultancy – after all, I'd had plenty of opportunity to stock up on management buzz-words, those being the days when 'buzz-word' still was a buzz-word; I knew the tax laws backwards; and a few 'how to' manuals from the stationery store supplied me with a passable line in off-the-peg homiletics. But I always made sure my name didn't appear on anything, however seemingly innocuous. You could say I'd learnt my lesson.

Yet what lesson had I learnt? Not one that helps me to understand why Ggarax ended up face down at the lakeside, his blood coiling away into the lapping waters like a red chiffon scarf... A chiffon scarf? In the stone age? A couple of weeks ago, on television, they did a programme about the French Revolution; and this commentator had a real cold sneer in his voice as he told us that Robespierre had been dragged to the guillotine screaming – no self-control, you see, no great last words, "It is a far, far better thing that I do now..." Yet I distinctly remember reading somewhere that Robespierre had had half his jaw shot away just before he was taken out to be executed, and that what was left of it had been quickly set back in place with sticky brown paper. I ask you – wouldn't you be screaming? It's been suggested he did it himself in a bungled attempt at suicide. But that doesn't hold water. How can you shoot yourself in the jaw if you're trying to blow your brains out? No, somebody wanted to make sure there'd be no speech from the scaffold. They were scared of him, that's why.

What made me think of that? Something to do with bosses, or prefects, or the red chiffon scarf. But on the subject of things in water, there's something that you may very well remember, because you were with me when I found it, and I've held onto it ever since. It's this piece of smoothed green stone. We were ambling along the foreshore of the river at low tide, and I saw it glinting, and at first I just assumed it had been worn into this gentle curve by the action of the waves rubbing it for centuries against the gravel. But as soon as I picked it up, and I saw the abrupt changes in the curvature, and the clean line where the curves intersected, I knew I'd found the remains of a neolithic axe. Not much of a specimen from a museum's point of view, as there's a fair chunk of it missing; but when I realised what it was, I stood there with it in my hand and I cried. Some people cry at slow music, or at characters dying in soap operas, and I've never felt the urge to; but now, for the first time in my adult life, because I was holding in my hand something that someone had made maybe 40,000 years ago, and I thought about the weeks it must have taken, maybe months, and the dedication, and the slow loving care, I stood there with tears rolling down my cheeks; and you came up and rubbed yourself against my leg and wagged your tail and looked up at me wondering what the trouble was. For a long time after that, I took all our walks along that foreshore, obsessively scanning the mud and probing it with a stick. I half hoped to find the missing piece of my axe in the vicinity; but then I realised it might have broken off so long ago as to be hundreds of miles away. Even so, I continued to nurse the hope of lighting upon another specimen. You got bored long before I did. The sharp stones in the muddy gravel were painful to your paws, and you soon settled for walking in parallel with me on the upper path. Rudekamp would have thought I'd gone potty. *They're coming to take you away, ha-ha, hee-hee, ho-ho*, the blokes would have sung.

And Fred Talcott – what would he have thought? He was always difficult to predict, which I suppose was why I took to him; and I ran into him quite frequently for a year or two after that encounter in the restaurant. We used sometimes to meet for a drink after work. He was a junior draughtsman with a firm of architects nearby, and spent his time mainly on drawings of details, which he'd have to copy from a standard pattern book – putting flesh on the bones of other people's creative doodles. Once he was offered some sort of promotion; but he turned it down on the grounds – or so he told me – that the work suited him, left him time to think his own thoughts. He had an old jalopy, falling apart; and he swore the reason he kept it was so that, if he were ever to be prosecuted for a driving offence, he'd be able to claim that it wasn't a vehicle within the meaning of the act. It was his humour I liked: dry, perhaps the right word would be 'mordant'. And that's something else that comes back to me. I once referred to something he'd said as 'gallows humour'; and he replied that, since we all know we're going to die, all humour is gallows humour. I laughed at that too. I was still relatively young.

Anyhow, I found nothing else on my riparian wanderings. Or if I did, I failed to recognise it as anything of interest. But I still keep the broken axe. It's one of my most valued possessions. Long after Ggarax's time, of course. So to get back to what I was saying: you can talk about sentimentality; but how can you possibly know how people felt about each other when there were scarcely any words in which to talk about it? Whatever stage language was at, they certainly wouldn't have had a word for 'sentimental'. Again, like the ancestry, it's a matter of definition. I'm not specifying dates; I'm just defining the period as one where language was teetering on that cusp between being just a kit of signals and being something you could think with. I dare say it teetered for a very long time. So for the moment, and in the absence of irrefutable evidence that the world of those days was modelled in Rudekamp's image, I'll stick with my little nymphs and shepherds scenario. I imagine Ggarax's fur dark and matted like that of a bison; but Kkinthe I see like one of those long-haired goats, cocoa and thick cream. Celia, that glacial secretary who – on a lucky day you'd get a glimpse – didn't shave her armpits: I'll never forget the time I caught a whiff of her under-arm odour, ancestral memory of Kkinthe's musk... Ggarax leads her gently to the heap of aromatic leaves that is their bed. He caresses her, then raises her onto her knees so he can enter her. When, I wonder, did people start doing it face-to-face? Perhaps it was less a matter of anatomical changes than of the advent of the concept of privacy: of being able to do it somewhere where you didn't have to keep constantly on the alert to see who might be creeping up on you with a rock in his hand. Then he gives her the present he has prepared for her: two lengths of hollow reed, each of which he has stoppered at one end with clay. She blows across them, and they make two sounds – a bit flaky, unclear, and not particularly pleasant to hear one after the other. They are no substitute for her lost swan-bones. He is disappointed in the poor quality of his present. But she, as she lies beside him, wrestles with a thought which she has difficulty in bringing into focus, yet which she is convinced is important. The two reeds are telling her something. They are telling her that two notes are not simply two notes: that it actually makes a difference which two notes they are. But how long may she have to search to find the two good ones again? Will such a fluke ever repeat itself?

Sometimes, without forewarning, my belly trembles. Spasms seem to ripple outward from some undisclosed epicentre. How appealing to think of one's bones being stored in small alcoves and accorded generations of respect!

I shall have to get up from this chair in a minute or two. What really frightens me is the suspicion that any ill-advised movement could serve to push this unnameable discomfort over into something far worse; and that once that has happened it will stay worse.

And you: how would you react to my discomforts? I know. You would peer at me with apparent sympathy, tipping your head to one side, then settle to await the commencement of some activity incontrovertibly dog-related.

THREE

Blood in the sky. Clotted clouds. Unwanted messages borne on silent wings. Strange that it should so match a dream I had deep in the night, which I think must have taken its cue from some clattering outside, where the tumbril was hauled down thronged streets, red hats of the sansculottes bobbing above the crowd as they accompanied it armed with pikestaffs to keep the populace at bay, and Robespierre's blood streaming like an uncoiled bandage from his damaged jaw – yes, I know it wouldn't have done, but that's how I dreamed it – and then it stopped in the square where the women were placidly knitting – mustn't forget the women knitting, though I think I added them on waking, and they're probably apocryphal anyway, down to Baroness Orczy at a guess – and a strange dreadful silence fell as Robespierre mounted the scaffold and it became apparent to all that, jaw or no jaw, he was going to make one final speech... What might he have said? It's a question I often return to in my more thoughtful moments. What can't be doubted is that, had it not been for his injury, he'd have made a splendid exit. They really did know, those people, how to keep up appearances to the very end. Their characters never faltered. Their masks never slipped, because – unlike people of our own benighted days – they truly believed in them. It's almost impossible to imagine what that must be like: to believe in your own image unto death, unfazed by circumstance.

Hup! two-three-four, hup! two-three-four... The old plates are giving me gyp today, just like when I'd got through my fortnight of more-or-less uninterrupted running on the spot, sleeping and waking – or so it seemed – and I could scarcely shuffle from the hut to the latrines and back. I reported sick on grounds of fallen arches, which caused hilarity without precedent among my hut-mates; but the medics took it seriously, brought in a bone-setter all the way from Salisbury, took casts so I could have arch supports made to measure, recommended plentiful cycling as exercise and arranged for me to be excused parades for three months: at which point, at last, and through no particular merit, I became an object of envy and admiration as someone who'd licked the system. Gradually my feet re-adjusted, and the pain went away. But I don't think physical damage – any more than mental damage – is ever really cured. It just bides its time, waits till your defences are weakened, then *Wham*!

You won't believe this, but I actually considered signing up for another seven years when my National Service came to an end. Gave it serious consideration. But then again, not all that serious, because I soon realised I was just being lulled into something. I'd got used to having my rudimen-tary needs looked after, and I enjoyed sipping ouzo under the fig tree – old enough to have supplied Adam and Eve with the basic decencies, I used to reckon – as I leaned against a stone wall wadded with decades of lime-wash and listened to the soft harshness of the conversation of people who didn't give a damn about enosis and just wanted to be left in peace to enjoy the company of their goats. But I knew full well that wasn't going to last. The parts would separate, as parts do, so you'd wonder suddenly where the whole had gone, if you hadn't just dreamed it: the days without malice in the banter; tolerance for the accumula-tion of 'possessions personal' within limits; the Count Basie orchestra on AFN... And for once I got it right. It wasn't long after my discharge that the ever-courteous, sun-dried locals started taking pot-shots at Tommies. Difficult to visualise, though. The main thing that comes to mind when I think of those people is their dowdy, hand-me-down,

1930s jackets mended and mended with unstinting devotion, presumably by their womenfolk.

Anyhow, it was back to what was beginning to be called the rat race. To be followed in due season by the fruits of exemplary labour: the house; Marge; you. You were Marge's idea, actually. She always claimed to love dogs, though she didn't like their 'left-behinds', as she called them; so it fell to me to deal with that aspect of your existence while her eyes were otherwise occupied. Did you love her, I wonder? Silly question; she fed you. And you're not likely to have been as exasperated as I was by her pelmets and her ruched covers and the fake mahogany pillar table for the telephone in the hall. "It's what you're supposed to have..." O Jesus, that table! Truly, when I think back on Marge, it's not her thighs I remember, or her tits, or any of the things a man's supposed to remember about a woman, not even the way her periods smelled of Brasso; it's that unspeakable pillar table with its slithery surface and its tendency to topple and its scalloped edges like the edges of her equally uncontroversial underwear, all guaranteed to please or money back. On one level, at least, it was conceived as being for my benefit. She was always nudging me to ask my bosses home to dinner, so that they could sip cocktails by the pool. You too, Doris: symbol of achieved domesticity. I used to try and explain to her that my bosses were of a different social stripe, and would be aghast if I were to invite them home; but she insisted that that was the done thing, it was how people won preferment, plying the bosses with hospitality, getting well in, crawling. Then one day she said to me, "You're not really interested in our life together, are you?" That stung, because I was forced to admit to myself that at rock bottom it was true, at least within the terms of her understanding. And my understanding? Well, I'm not sure I understood anything much in those days. *You're not paid to think, sonny...* and that was how it went. But one thing's for certain: I never told Marge about our little moment of triumph, you and I, with the cricketer on the common. The idea of discomfiting the rich and pompous was not to her taste. The rich had a right to be pompous – because they were rich – and it was childish to alienate those whose favours you would need to rely upon if you were ever to get anywhere in life. Rudekamp's philosophy, that no-one was going to do you any favours but yourself, and that life was exclusively a matter of who kicks whom in the goolies first, she would have considered ill-bred. As for Bborog, she'd have wanted me to ask him round for dinner.

I wonder though, on reflection, whether I haven't always oversimplified Rudekamp's position. In fairness, I don't think he was a sadist. He didn't actively enjoy hurting people. He just thought that it was something you had to do, and there was no point in being squeamish about it. That's a distinction that's hard to make when you're the victim; but it may be that he was closer to Robespierre than I've ever realised; and of course, the distinction was rather lost on his victims too. Rudekamp, it seems clear to me now, had become aware of the thinness of the veneer of democratic chatter that covers the brutalities of social life; but having seen through it, rather than denounce it in the name of something better, he treated it as a game in which his insight into its nature would lend him significant advantage. So what did Robespierre do, then? Did he denounce hypocrisy in the name of something better? It would be easy to settle for that as a rough outline; but I'm not sure it quite gets there. Rudekamp, that last occasion, weaving away between the tables as he left, calling back over his shoulder as I made my way to the gents, "Look after your bloody bladder, then!": at all costs he had to have the last word; but having the last word meant keeping the game in play, reaffirming the rules even among people who didn't know them, afraid of what might lie outside their cosy ambit, perhaps: *Here Be Terrors*. Robespierre, they say, signed death warrants with tears in his eyes. They say that about all tyrants, of course; but we can only go on the Robespierre we know. And that would not have struck Rudekamp as manly. But Robespierre was aware of something which, though it's implicit in Rudekamp's model of human relations, Rudekamp himself never spotted because the model subtly deflects attention from it: namely, that nobody ever takes revenge upon the powerful. It's not just political rebels. Even common murderers, almost without exception, kill only those weaker and poorer than themselves. It's surely a taboo as deeply rooted in our history as the taboo against incest. That's why Ggarax had to triumph over Bborog by side-stepping him, not by creeping up at night and smashing his brains out. And that's exactly the taboo Robespierre was out to destroy, because it offended against reason. The privileged and the powerful would be sent to the guillotine – murdered not even furtively, but in the full light of day. And he wept as he signed the death warrants so as never to forget, never to let waver, his status as the weak wreaking vengeance upon the strong.

At the time I got the push from Feal & Divot, Marge somehow managed to twist the scenario so I could be represented as having been guilty of excessive scruple: "You always had to ask questions, couldn't take a hint. It's the bosses that were running that firm, not you; but you wouldn't accept that..." I just kept quiet. I can only process elementary data. I remember watching her glistening red lips as they metamorphosed endlessly, like some plankton-sifting water nymph, while retaining a broad symmetry.

When the hire car came to fetch her – she was standing

in a little desert atoll of matching pigskin suitcases – she gave me a last hug and said she'd write. Perhaps it was just that she didn't know what the hell else to say. It's probably not a situation for which Emily Post provides. Still, there was something in her look almost hesitant, almost humane: something which transported me right back to the time I'd first known her, so that I began faintly to remember what it had been that had attracted me to her all those years before. But I'd more sense than to take her up on any half-imagined offer of reconciliation. I strolled back into the echoey house, poured myself a nameless cocktail and stood gazing out of the French windows at the scummy pool – and beyond it, under the trees, unmarked, your burial place. She never did write.

Robespierre, it occurs to me, was the only politician, in Europe at least, who's ever been on the side of the oppressed. I mean *really* on our side. All right, maybe he went off the rails a bit towards the end. But then think of the stress he must have been under. Someone of greater personal warmth would never have held on that long. The question is, though, whether his was the only way, or whether something can be learned from Ggarax's example. Once, when I'd become embroiled in a particularly sticky correspondence with the IR, I began to notice an odd pattern of behaviour. Whenever I scored an unanswerable point against my opposite number, I would receive a reply not to that but to my previous letter. Eventually I grasped the significance. He was concerned for his file. He was concerned that, should his overseer do a spot check on his correspondence, he must not be seen to have been placed at a disadvantage; and he was therefore destroying any letter that showed him to be in the wrong. So, having found out the overseer's name, I sent him a photocopy of the complete correspondence with the comment that I did not seem to be making myself understood. Within two days the matter was resolved. I suppose you'd call that boxing clever. All the same, you make enemies; and I've wondered latterly whether my eventual fall from grace hadn't been longer in fermentation than I ever suspected at the time. In any case, I had not really side-stepped the hierarchy. I had merely exploited another group's hierarchy to my own advantage. How easy can it be to find a loophole in a system solidified by untold generations of evolutionary compulsion? As a dog, you'll understand such things – even without knowing that your own evolution has been largely human-directed. And I'm taking it for granted that questions of status will be of interest to you, though in human discourse it's 'not done' to mention them.

Broad noses twitch. Eyes glitter blackly in the leaf-shadow. Ears are alert for the thud of heavy feet or the rough scrunch of foliage. Hands tense around lumps of shaped stone... But no, it's too soon for this. Something has to have happened first...

She'd never have understood – Marge – I'm convinced: never have learned to inquire what goes on below the scum of things. D'you happen to remember that dinner party we had when I'd invited Fred Talcott and another of my old mates from Limassol whom Fred was still in touch with, Dickie Chalmers – now sporting a nifty moustache? And Chalmers's wife, she came too. At first we were all a bit stiff and formal; but then the three of us blokes lapsed gradually into the mode of reminiscence. First we talked about what a pig Rudekamp had been. Then we turned to the inexhaustible subject of army food: "Well, you know what they used to say. Army cooks never make shepherd's pie. It just accumulates..." Marge tried to guide the conversation onto more sedate topics; but Dickie's wife wasn't much help, being one of those women who smile indulgently at everything hubbie says; and we were soon back on track with the evergreen question of whether it was really true they put bromide in the tea to stop you getting horny. Finally, with a sort of horrible inevitability, we arrived at the subject of cures for venereal diseases: "And this guy, he reported sick with a dose of the clap, and the MO says to him, 'All right, this time you can have penicillin; but come back with the same again and it's the umbrella for you, my lad.'" And Marge – as you are my witness, Doris, I did try to avert this when I saw it coming – she asked what the umbrella was; and, with as much delicacy as the subject allowed, he told her. While Dickie's wife was giggling herself senseless, Marge got up and, with commendable dignity, left the table. We all waited, expecting her to reappear with the dessert; but eventually it dawned on me that she wasn't going to. In fact she'd left the house altogether – walked out into the street in her dinner party dress. So I went to serve out the dessert myself, which was to be pears in chocolate sauce. The tins of pears were neatly lined up with the opener laid across them. The sauce was coagulating in the pan. And for no reason at all it came back to me: peering down into that bath. When you straighten after a caning, a wave of nausea hits you and you want to throw up. I managed to resist giving my tormentors that satisfaction – a triumph I cherish, worthless as it is. But now, for the first time, I found myself wondering about those yellow-brown encrustations: was it conceivable that generations of vomit had been allowed to accumulate and coagulate as testimony to the power of discipline: the sort of thing the upper classes call a 'tradition'?

Marge came home late that night and slept on the sofa downstairs. I didn't entirely blame her. Yet the truth is that she'd been turned off by the manner and missed a good deal of the substance of the event. Once the common ground of recollection had been affirmed, which meant the common ground of anecdote, then less predictable things could be explored in safety. When the conversation came round to what sort of literature we kept on our bedside tables, Marge would have been surprised to hear Fred Talcott say he never slept without a copy of *The Rubaiyat of Omar Khayyam* within reach. So was I. Fred was always a loner, an almost monkish type; and that he should somehow have found support for his asceticism in the sybaritic poetry of Khayyam struck me as something to be thought about. But before I could come to grips with that, Dickie Chalmers was replying that his own choice of bedside book was *Julius Caesar*; and when asked why, he said, "So's I never fall into the mistake of forgiving them."

Right. It is early morning. The sky is liverish. Ggarax is concerned for Kkinthe, who is experiencing occasional pains. Is this the beginning? Is she all right? Are things as they should be? He doesn't know. Neither does she, as it is her first. But from her size he thinks it must come soon. She ought to be taken to the birthing hut. Therefore he must go to the axe-maker.

Watchful, Ggarax goes alone up the narrowing defile. It has taken him half the morning to cross the plain, through grass ever coarser, with an eye always for where the grass might betray some movement that was not of the wind. It is not good for one person to go so far alone. It isn't often done. He said to others, "Kkinthe near birth. Going to axe-maker. Come." But they all said, "Bborog say big hunt. Kkinthe wait." Ggarax did not wait. He thought: Hunt any time; Kkinthe need axe-maker. Now, having reached the river and turned towards its source, he must be alert for threat from overhead as the sides of the gulley close in and he has to clamber over fallen trees which become more and more numerous, and creepers are thick and plentiful, and the bared rock walls are wet and frightening. The final climb is almost vertical up the flue of a small but strong waterfall. At the top is a calm pool of water waiting its turn to tipple over the stone lip; and beyond that, in a rocky glade, is the cave where the axe-maker lives alone. He lives alone because axe-makers, like women at certain times and especially at the time of birthing, are unclean. Their uncleanness reflects their engagement in processes which, though necessary to the wellbeing of the species, conflict with the common ordering of life. Not everyone can make an axe, or would wish to spend all his days so doing, any more than a child can be produced just when wanted without any disruption of domesticity. That is why only an axe-maker can attend to a woman's needs, and to her protection, once she is ready for the birthing hut.

Ggarax halts in the entranceway of the cave, peering across the scattered débris to where the axe-maker sits beside a small pile of hand axes, all resolutely identical, gently prising fine flakes from the edge of a flint with a piece of impala horn. He does not look up until he is ready. Then Ggarax says, "Woman near birthing;" and he adds: "My woman." The axe-maker rises, selects from a neat pile behind him a hand-axe to his satisfaction, then limps forward to join Ggarax. "We go," he says. He says nothing more. His limp offers little impediment to his movement, and by evening the two men have reached the settlement. There is no sign of a hunt having taken place. Bborog, seated on his bed-heap and being groomed by three compliant women, does not deign to look in their direction. They pause to eat some dried apple slices from an almost exhausted supply which Kkinthe has kept in a hare-skin since last autumn, then set off for the hut – little more than an extra-strong lean-to against a big fig tree – a few hundred yards away. When they are nearly there, Ggarax stops. He must approach no further. Kkinthe and the axe-maker go on alone. The hut is in disrepair, as it is some time since the last birth, and the axe-maker sets about cutting new branches to roof it and fresh growth for the bed. He also cuts a straight spear for himself. He will spend his nights in the tree, keeping watch, but will sound a general alarm only in case of attack by large predators. In the daytime he will come to the settlement to beg food for her, or will perhaps do some fishing or trapping on his own account. He will sleep little, and only fitfully, until the birth is accomplished. If the birth is unsuccessful, he will be chased away with sticks and with heavy beatings. If it is successful, he will not be included in the celebrations and will slink back to his cave. If he failed to perform this duty, it is to be assumed that the people would cease to bring him food in exchange for his axes, and would find a new axe-maker or appoint one from among their number. But it is difficult to say, since no axe-maker has ever put it to the test by declining his given function.

All this is poppycock, of course. I know it is, because I'm constantly finding myself obliged to paper over contradictions of one sort and another. I invented the dried apples because I couldn't think what there'd be to eat if there hadn't been a hunt – and, as I've been envisaging these events taking place in early summer, I couldn't resort to nuts or fruit without cheating. So then, having rustled up the dried apples, I had to posit some container for people who wouldn't have had cloth or pottery: hence the hare-skin pouch. The truth is that it's very difficult to imagine any complex social activity, involving rituals, technical specialisations – even speech of any significant sort – without dragging in the whole shebang: in effect, neolithic culture. So you can see why it had to happen: because it was overwhelmingly difficult for it not to. Still, never mind.

Let's see what we can make of the hunt.

They're waiting. They're listening. They are stationed in the undergrowth either side of a trampled path which funnels gently towards a gap between two big rocks. They are upwind of where the rhinoceros has been sighted, where the grasses are more dense; and it will catch their scent soon. Its trampling feet are audible. Suddenly, a long way off, it is there. Woolly, needless to say. Someone walks into full view and waves his arms. The rhinoceros snorts once or twice, swings its heavy head sullenly from side to side, takes a few steps forward, pauses, then breaks into a trot. The man turns and runs, and the rhino speeds into an insistent rhythm to give chase. Soon both are going as fast as they can, and the ground shudders under the rhino's gallop. As the man senses that his pursuer is uncomfortably close, he darts to one side and into the undergrowth, across-wind from the beast, vanishing almost instantly from its weak sight; but as he does so, and before the rhino can check its enormous momentum, another man pops into view, 30 or 40 yards on, and takes up the action. It is the fourth of these men, acting in relay, who leads the rhino between the two rocks and leaps with ease over the trench they have dug in preparation. The trench is neither wide nor deep; but it is sufficient to catch the fore-legs of a rhinoceros coming at full velocity. As the animal falls, Ggarax and two companions rush towards it with a heavy spear, its point fire-hardened, which they must force with all their combined strength into the blood vessel of its neck. Ggarax, in the lead, bears the main responsibility for the accuracy of their aim. He is good at it. But at that very moment he hears, from the direction of the birthing hut, a two-note interval repeated three times. He is distracted. He misses his aim. Others crowd forward brandishing hand-axes and spears just as the rhinoceros begins thrashing around wildly in an attempt to get to its feet. A hind leg catches Ddonod on the shin, and you can hear the crack as it breaks. He shrieks. The others scatter as the rhino charges blindly in their general direction then charges away into the undergrowth. The stunned silence that follows is broken by the roar of Bborog. He turns towards Ggarax: "He think woman. Now Ddonod damaged. No food for all!" Ggarax has already turned and fled into the bushes, weaving expertly yet with desperation this way and that, as he hears the cry taken up: "No more Ggarax! No more Ggarax!"

Well, we know how it ends – perhaps hours later, perhaps next day, because he does not want to stray too far from Kkinthe – with Ggarax face down in the shallows, his blood curling away from him like a red chiffon scarf... I wish I could tell you what the dogs were doing, but I can't.

So that's it. Something achieved. I had the foresight to make myself coffee before embarking on that story; but I forgot to drink it, and now it's cold. Time for some serious nosh. Rhinoceros is off, though. And again I fall to wondering when will be the first time that I'm not fit enough to go out and replenish necessities. What will happen then? Shall I starve? It's so simple. What happened to Ddonod? Did they just leave him there? How the hell should I know? It's all make-believe, as I said before: only a matter of trying to figure out how things *might* have happened – because what's beyond doubt is that they happened somehow, and we did get here in the end. If you call this the end. I went to the doctor to hear the results of my tests. He said, "It's likely to be quite some months yet before you're in need of sedation. Best make the most of it." I said, "You mean before the pain gets so bad...?" He kept his head down, looking at his papers, as he nodded; then, as if ashamed of this evasion, he looked up and met my eye; and he gave a sort of rueful smile and a faint, sad shrug, as if to say, "It comes to us all eventually."

Decent bunch, the medics. They fixed up my feet. But you can't expect miracles.

So I'm left wondering how to 'make the most of it.' Should I, even at this late stage, make efforts to track down those three prefects so as to shadow them, one by one, until the moment comes to snap the command "Cross now!" – ? What happened to them, I wonder? Did they become circuit judges with shady connections, quangocrats burdened with needy families? The truth is, they weren't so very different from everybody else. But does that exonerate them? I'm reminded of something Rudekamp said when I'd met him that time in the street. He was reminiscing about his own schooling, and telling me how, when they rapped your knuckles with a ruler, "They didn't just thwack you with it casually but slammed the ruler down flat, parallel to the desk surface, like I once saw a policeman do to a kaffir with the barrel of a thirty-eight. Man, they really hated you in those days..."

Even you bit me once – and I was trying to help you, too. You'd tried to jump over a neighbour's garden gate, probably in chase of a squirrel, and had somehow caught your rear leg in the ironwork, and were hanging there wriggling and yelping. Without thinking, worried that you might do yourself some real damage, I rushed over and yanked your leg out of its trap; and you turned and bit my hand. For weeks I had a great purple and yellow bruise, and thought perhaps I ought to get the bone X-rayed; but it cleared up eventually. You were terribly apologetic, I recall. Ironical, really.

Come to think of it, there was something a little dog-like about Fred Talcott. I'm not talking about the qualities people quote as typically canine – loyalty, devotion – but more of the way he seemed to occupy any space in which he found himself as if by natural right; or rather – because 'right' scarcely came into it – in the way a species can occupy an evolutionary niche, in much the way you used to occupy the doorstep or the corner by the stove. He could fit in unobtrusively. As a conscript, he could dress neatly "if," as he used to say, "that's what pleases their little minds." He was a good shot – the sort that makes it easy to forget the purpose of shooting. I don't know how he coped with basic training, because he wasn't part of our intake; but I'm pretty sure he had no experience of disciplinary proceedings, CO's orders. We all thought of him as some sort of an anarchist; but his rebellion, if it was rebellion, was something as deeply bedded in his nature as doghood in yours, expressed only in the way he walked, the way he smiled, the way he waited for events to work themselves out.

I'm tired already.

Hup! two-three-four... At the double...

Or quits.

How many cups of coffee have I drunk in my life? How many times have I sat in a deck-chair enjoying a good thriller? How often, watching you cavorting through the long grass, have I reflected that life is worth living in spite of everything? It's time now to summon these memories: time, as Christians used to say, for the reckoning of the accounts. Once, on holiday in Ramsgate, I tried to knap a flint into an axe-head. But I was crap at it.

I was talking about that axe-head we found in the river, wasn't I? It's still on my desk. It still affects me with a sort of temporal vertigo. But in other respects, sadly, it doesn't carry the meaning it once had for me. A book from the local library put me right: and I now know that, far from being the product of loving labour, the thing was almost certainly turned out by some half-starved creature on piece rates in a sweatshop at Penwith or Graig Lwyd. Yes, the rot had set in by then. But when hadn't it?

FOUR

A buffeted sky: clouds piled high and streaked with buttercup. A sky full of triumph and irony. And another purely ceremonial erection – which makes two in a week. At one time in my life I'd have been ashamed; at another, proud. Now it means no more to me than my old ready-reckoner – cloth-bound, greasy, dog-eared – which I kept out of sentiment after decimalisation, only to discover that sentiment – which I'd supposed a sturdy weed – dies back, like everything else, in what my Mum would have called God's good time. It is a form of mercy, I suppose. The question is, what's left?

It's a while now since I heard, by a roundabout route, that Marge had died. Cancer of some vital organ. I never found out which, and it scarcely matters. Occasionally I imagine her buried by your side under the flowering cherry, her mound eventually subsiding as yours must have done because all mounds do in time. After all, we did share something, didn't we, the three of us? And downstairs in your basket you must, I'm sure, have twitched an ear at the bed-spring accompaniment to our increasingly infrequent couplings. What's 'is-name – what *was* his name? – seated on the edge of a bunk obsessively oiling his rifle, sliding the bolt to and fro... We all knew what he was thinking. But we never took the mickey; because we were wise enough to know by then that you can't always have what life owes you... Which reminds me, I spotted Fred Talcott the other day, walking along the opposite side of the street in a long brown overcoat with – or so I imagined – *Omar Khayyam* in an inside pocket, snug against his heart. His hair had gone grey, but he still smiled his secret smile as he must have been smiling it all the days of his life, the smile of one who understands other people's actions and is amused in a sympathetic way by their weaknesses, the smile of one who knows promotion is a pointless encumbrance since we're all going to snuff it in the end. And all at once I saw the connection between the Omar Khayyam and the faded, desolate quality of his being. He is a man who, right from the start, saw the future and knew it would never work: and that is why he believes in seizing the moment; but it is also why he can never be bothered to do so. I was on the point of calling out to him, but I didn't; and then I realised I didn't want to. Gallows humour has lost its allure.

Already the buttercup has gone, and the triumph with it. The sky is merciful. That is what it's for: to dissolve all things, whether triumphs or powder compacts or old uniforms or the Bay of Akrotiri trembling like hot tin at noon: to dissolve them, and to stir the pain into the broth too, so as to offer always the hope that it will reform them into new patterns, new enactments. Enactments? Let it stand. I bear the sorry burden of the autodidact, which is never to have been taught what it's all right to think about; and I shall bear it until I join that patient queue of the dead facing back to the time when we set up Stonehenge with such reckless, all-vanquishing optimism – and beyond that the longer queue back, back, back to Ggarax and Kkinthe...

All at once I realise what the fleeting figure of Fred Talcott put me in mind of with his long brown coat: an illustration by Arthur Rackham in one of those fairytale books that had belonged to my father and my Mum could never bring herself to chuck away: an illustration of some benevolent goblin or simian wizard walking against a resistance of finely-spun cobweb. Eventually, of course, I chucked the books out myself. That was at a time in life when it seemed imperative to look to the future.

Years ago, in one of the weekend supplements, I read about an experiment they'd done with rats. They'd put these rats in a maze – in London, let's say – and recorded the time it took them to learn it so's they could go through it without any errors. Then they did the same thing, with an identical maze, somewhere on the other side of the world; and they found that the rats learned the route in half the time. They concluded that knowledge gained by one group of rats somehow spread to all other rats, irrespective of distance. I didn't believe a word of it. But now I've no choice. Haven't you ever wondered why people don't just give up, just switch their extravagant brains off and stop thinking at all when it's obvious that their thoughts can't hope to be of any consequence or even to reach anybody beyond themselves? We never do. We go on to the bitter end following where the words lead us, puzzling over things that nobody's asked us to puzzle over, addressing problems already solved a dozen times, pouring our diminishing energies into unproductive effort. The only way of justifying this is to believe in the story of the rats. Very well: once again I lay out the contents of my mind before me on the pavement and try to interest the passers-by... "Stone axe, guv'nor – genuine neolith – hand-crafted by experts to the highest standards; state-of-the-art for its time; *Vorsprung durch Technik...*"

Yesterday I was depressed, and I found myself being a touch negative about this axe-head. Fair enough up to a point; but there was something I wasn't taking into account, and it came to me when I woke up in the early hours: we're talking here about a pre-literate society. Well, why should that make a difference? Good question. I think it comes down to something like this. If you try to imagine a society where nothing could be written down, where you knew that every thought however fascinating, every insight however profound, was going to die either with you or, at best, with someone you'd told it to, and at worst would be forgotten by all of you within a week or two, it's actually very hard to get to grips with: hard to think yourself into a situation where every product of your brain was insubstantial as thistledown, ready to blow away in an instant. The exception was physical objects. Those would last – perhaps for a very long time. In fact maybe the realisation that an artifact might survive you was the first thing to introduce humanity to the concept of personal immortality. In which case, even the product of sweated labour becomes a thing of joy. Ask again what exactly they were doing when they built Stonehenge. We think of it as either an observatory or a temple: something that was perhaps meant to generate ideas, or was perhaps a monument to ideas. But I think the truth of the matter is that Stonehenge *was* the ideas – in exactly the same way that a jostle of equations on a blackboard *is* the ideas it expresses, rather than simply a homage to them or a tool for using them. All right; but still, why drag all those massive sarsens for miles over Salisbury plain? Why did it have to be so damn big? We usually assume it was to impress the yokels; and I dare say word had reached them of what the Rameses family were up to out east. Yet I still can't quite believe that the thinking behind Stonehenge was to create something like an Albert Speer triumphal arch – that it was meant to impress in quite our present-day, theatrical sense. No, I think the stones had to be heavy because they were our thoughts; and the heavier they were, the less the fear that they'd blow away like thistledown. And the same goes for that charnel house at West Kennet, generations earlier; except that here it wasn't a question of thoughts being held fast: it was the dead themselves. In the weight of the stones the dead would find permanence. That's why there weren't any ghosts at West Kennet. It's taken me all these years to work that out. Ghosts are what happen when the dead are conceived as transient, as fleeting, as touching our world only tentatively. West Kennet was spookless not because the dead had departed but because they were still there.

So that's something else achieved, don't you agree? There are those who'd query whether telling stories to a dead dog was the ideal way for a man under sentence to 'make the most of' the time remaining to him. But you see, we've actually reached a conclusion on a question of real substance. And what would be the point, at this stage in my life, of dissipating my attention onto glamorous new projects? Better I should devote myself to tying up the loose ends of the teasers that have been occupying me – and trust the rest to the rats.

Be patient, old Doris, as you always were. I've got the end in view now. Perhaps it's my dereliction in the offspring stakes that makes it seem particularly important I should set these matters in order. No-one to take over the family concern...

Does that mean, then, that our conclusions re Stonehenge, the axe-head and West Kennet resolve the questions I was addressing through the person of Ggarax? Not quite; but the particular problems of pre-literacy help me to identify just what it was I was reaching for on the more general level. Take it this way. Scientists are for ever banging on about the fact that evolution is purposeless, purely reactive and mechanical, and above all not concerned to find means for fashioning human excellence from the primal crud. The idea is not so difficult for us to grasp as most scientists seem to imagine. But the more readily I accept it, the more strange it seems that this purely causal process, with no eye to the future it is prosecuting, should have given rise to an organism which can envisage futurity and which – 'free will' doesn't enter into this – understands itself as acting so as to bring about this or that future event. In a very real sense, the future did not exist until the human mind gave birth to it. Nothing else, and certainly not evolution, has known that there might be such a thing. Clearly language must have been responsible. And that is the revelation I was looking for. A sunrise so slow that it took perhaps half a million years; yet there must have been a moment when someone first formulated the concept 'tomorrow', or said, "We don't have this now, but will have it later." That, to me, is the miracle of life on Earth. And what did we do with this miraculous light of unfulfilledness, this unprecedented perspective into the chasm of the universe's potential? I'll tell you what we did with it: we gave it to Bborog. We said with one voice: "I can't bear the intensity, I can't bear the knowledge of all that unformed time to come, I can't bear knowing I am part of the causal chain that will inexorably form it, I am afraid of what I might do. Please, Bborog, take this responsibility from me." So he did. Gladly. Bborog, of course, could not face the light either; but he wasn't telling. It was sufficient for him that he was being offered authority, and with it the perks of authority: not the least of which is unconditional moral absolution.

On the other hand, perhaps it did not happen like that. The transaction may have been clouded by the fact that, being apes, we inherited a ready-formed command structure. The significance of Ggarax may be that he was the first to challenge that. Certainly he's turned out to have been one of few. And he did it for Kkinthe; that must not be overlooked: Kkinthe, in whose two swan's-bone notes it would – I suppose – be absurd to imagine she found an intimation of the harmony of the heavens. Does it not seem, then, that Mills and Boon have been right all along, and that love must inevitably win out? In that case, how do we explain the persistence of the taboo? For God's sake, it's not just that we never kill the rich and powerful, we don't even like to see them humiliated. Imagine it had been a major-general who'd pissed the bed: there'd have been no lewd laughter then! Oh yes, people would have whispered the news to each other; but it would have been in a tone of shocked awe amounting in some twisted way even to an enhanced reverence.

So then...

People mill around with fearsome knives stuffed into their belts and tricolour cockades in their hats. Guardsmen form a frail ring, bayonets fixed, backs to the machine of retribution from whose vicinity the knitting women have, on this special occasion, been evicted. A wheelwright, leaning against his doorpost, is softly whistling *Ça Ira*, a tune whose first and third lines are composed of only two notes. Amazing how far you can get with just two notes! A restless silence falls – in which for a moment those two notes are exposed, laid bare – as the tumbril is heard approaching, all squeaks and rumbles. The authorities are nervous because the plan to maim Robespierre before his execution has misfired. He climbs from the cart onto the scaffold, which creaks even with his slender weight, having been left out too long in the weather, submitted to too many hard thuds. Neat and spruce, he still affects the dress of the class he has done so much to eradicate – for our dress codes lie deeper than our ideologies. He is no popular orator; more of an attorney, a demon for the detail; more a rapier than a bludgeon. But whatever his talents, he will have to make the best he can of them this time.

"Citizens..." He clears his throat and begins again: "Citizens, I greet you in the name of the Revolution which you, and I, and many dear friends now parted, have brought to its present glory and to which I now willingly surrender my own life." The authorities relax – though only fractionally. He is not going to plead with the mob to overthrow the judgment. But if not that, what? He's a clever one, no doubt about it...

"I scarcely need tell you, my comrades in struggle, how earnestly I have laboured to enact the will of the people – nay, to embody it – or how heavily have weighed upon me the setbacks of recent months. True to our enlightened age, I confess to my errors, if only so that those who come after may learn from them and avoid them; and the greatest of these was my failure to foresee the enormity of the resistance that would be mounted against the reign of hope and brotherly love. Naturally we expected opposition from those whose unearned riches we confiscated, whose untilled land we distributed to the deserving, whose boot we rudely dislodged from the necks of the humble – although even they, we allowed ourselves to think, might in time see the justice of our acts and look beyond their immediate deprivation to a future of fraternal equality, a future when man would no longer be set against man like dogs in a pit but would be free to share together in the enjoyment of the earth's bounty."

The soldiers are finding it increasingly difficult to ignore the gaze of the crowd they confront. Their silence, their immobility, seem to pose a danger more profound than would outward signs of disaffection.

"Yes, we expected opposition from those formerly privileged. What we did not expect was the alliance of so many of the common people with their oppressors, the failure to grasp what had been clearly explained, the petty antagonisms at every level, the bestial concern for individual wellbeing that led to the hoarding of foodstuffs while others hungered, the defection in the face of the foreign invader of generals who owed their very rank to our revolutionary government and to the honest people whom their actions betrayed, the failure of even the most dedicated and loyal to understand the measures which had to be taken in the face of such catastrophic threats to the very heart of our just cause..."

Robespierre's captors glance at each other with uncertainty. They cannot stop him now; but someone must be ready to rebut his statements if he seems on the point of swaying the mob – whose mood remains unfathomable. The executioner must be ready to act swiftly while the Guards hold back the people should they attempt to storm the scaffold.

"But here is where I must confess to my second and greater error. In my zeal to defend what we had won from the onslaughts of our enemies, I allowed myself to become more than your representative – more, even, than the representative of those who did not believe I represented their true interests. I allowed myself to fall into the habit of being obeyed uncritically. I allowed myself to become a leader. It is not what I sought; it is not what I ever wished; but I nonetheless allowed it to happen. No-one, my fellow-citizens, should defer as a matter of principle or of mindless habit to the authority of another. Why else did we overthrow our aristocracy and our priests? Obedience is the enemy of the future."

A sanseoulotte prods a Guardsman in the chest with the brown, juicy stem of his clay pipe and growls, "I hope you're listening to this, mate."

"I cannot but consent to accept the logic of my own acts. And it is in this spirit that I welcome my death here today; for it is the death which must rightly come to all who wield power over others. But let it not end with me. My last request – and I ask it humbly of you in the name of the great movement we have set in train together – is that you should remain forever vigilant, and bring to this place in their turn any who offend as I have done."

There is a murmur from the crowd as Robespierre kneels to rest his neck on the lower stock of the guillotine and peers down into the basket where, among a tangle of bloody hair and a smell of butchery, he meets the sightless eyes of Saint-Just, Sergeant Rudekamp and another, fresher, unrecognised, whose lips struggle lunglessly to frame the words, "Cross now..." The murmur lifts to a great roar; and those who have brought the victim here, realising after a moment's bemused hesitation that by assuming his mantle on the terms specified they will ensure their own eventual beheading, slope off shrugging and muttering amid a squad of bodyguards. The executioner, left behind on the scaffold, does the only thing a sane man could do under these circumstances: rips off his black mask, raises a clenched fist and yells at the top of his voice, "Vive Saint Maximilien!" Soon Robespierre, stunned by the abruptness of the reversal, is being carried shoulder high back to the Assembly. Washer-women strew his path with lilies. It will only be a year or two before he crowns himself emperor amid an adulatory multitude in the church of Notre Dame. He has won because he has lost; or perhaps lost because he has won.

All right, just a little parable, a thought experiment, a fancy. I'd hate you to think I'd started taking myself seriously at this late hour. Besides, you wouldn't stand much chance commending policies like that to the powers that be – I mean policies like judicious culling of the powerful. And perhaps we must accept that it would be inhumane to kill our bosses, even though we know they never have the slightest compunction about killing us. Perhaps a more moderate solution, a Girondin solution if you like, might be advanced: that anyone who wishes to assume a position of power – policeman, Lord Protector, managing director of a multinational conglomerate – should be allowed to do so on condition he or she consents to be sterilised, and for his or her children, if such be already spawned, to be sterilised too. Most power-seekers would probably consider that a tolerable price to pay for their own apotheosis; and by this means the characteristics of leadership and vainglory might, by selective breeding over an extended period, be eliminated from our species. The deferential, being left with no-one to whom to defer, would wither into insignificance and, finding themselves able to do no more harm, lose interest in life altogether.

Is this the end, then? I suppose so. I've no end of endings. I'm still not sure, though, about Ggarax and Kkinthe. There's a nagging feeling of something left unsaid. How many tunes do you suppose the average person knows? Hymns remembered from school assembly, pop songs, ballads, jingles, snatches from the classics: it must stretch into the hundreds, even for someone who isn't particularly musical. Yet what is a tune? It's nothing but a succession of intervals, of arithmetical ratios between frequencies. That's all. How extraordinary, then, that we should have the compulsion to memorise such sequences. Of course, you may say we're not memorising the mathe-matics, we're memorising the tunes; but, since the ratios are all there is, it seems to me we should be saying that tunes are the way the human brain memorises mathematics. So what evolutionary advantage...? And now I realise what I overlooked. When Kkinthe went to the birthing hut, she didn't have the swan's bones with her. The two notes Ggarax heard at the climax of the attack on the rhinoceros were not blown over pipes: they were pitched with the voice. That was what made Ggarax miss his aim.

The skyline is a uniform grey. The grey of ouzo. It wasn't so much the flavour I liked about ouzo as that deli-cate greyness: the misty swirl when you added the water. It used to remind me of fog around the Elephant. But there aren't any fogs in London anymore – just a soup of scarcely visible toxicity, a urine-tinged atmosphere.

I sit here endlessly reciting my multiplication tables, just to reassure myself I haven't forgotten them. I would garland the hours with sexual fantasy, were it not for the slight distaste aroused in me by the recognition that most of the women with whom I've customarily fantasised sex – hairy Celia, to name but one – have probably been dead for years.

Here's a little poem my old Mum used to recite to me:

I'm leaving you, my lovely
I'm leaving you for good
While all the donkeys in the town
Are braying as they should...

I don't remember the rest of it. I do remember, though, the day your puppies were born. For weeks you'd been getting heavier and heavier, until your hindquarters lost all suppleness and moved in one mass as if made of wood. Then one day, moving across a shaft of sunlight on the bare, sanded boards, you paused and began panting; and from your rear you expelled an unbroken sac as if a child had blown a bubble through hooped fingers at bathtime, and inside it was a tiny blind black dog. You waddled forward, seemingly indifferent. Then the umbilicus stretched and broke, and the sac tore, and the fluids soaked into the floorboards and the puppy gave an almost inaudible little yelp; and at that point your ears pricked up and you turned with an expression of transcendental joy such as I would not have believed could have registered on a dog's face; and you took the puppy between your lips, carried it to your nest and began licking it. And then you gave birth to another seven, two of which were dead.

Everyone told us we would have to drown a couple more of them, because you'd never be able to provide milk for them all, especially as it was your first time, and they'd all become sickly, and you'd become worn out, so that more of them would die in the long run. And I guess they were probably right, because even of the four we left I once caught you behaving very threateningly towards the youngest. Yes, that was my adored little Fruit Bat, whom I used to hold in one hand to rub noses with. I was watching as she tumbled around the food bowl with the others, being buffeted and bundled to one side although there was plenty to eat; and suddenly you rushed at her snarling and growling, and chased her away from the food; and when she tried pathetically to return, you snatched her by the scruff as if you were about to shake her like a rabbit and kill her. I didn't wait to find out, but shrieked at you to stop. You dropped the puppy, which limped away as if dazed; and you turned and gave me a look which is almost indescribable, and which I have never forgotten. 'If only they could speak...' It really was like that. You obviously weren't sure whether we, as your owners, had the right to override your instinctual deprivation of the runt, a long canine tradition of proven efficacy in the fight for survival. 'Well, I suppose they do supply the food,' you might have been thinking, 'so perhaps it's up to them to decide...' However your thoughts might have been formulating themselves – or might not, more likely – there was not the slightest doubt that I was witness to something extraordinary as a comet or an eclipse, and still more extraordinary than your look of joy at the recognition that you'd given birth. I was seeing a dog confront an ethical dilemma.

You never attacked Fruit Bat again. Nevertheless, holding those small creatures – little, muscular, suede-covered pumping hearts, they felt like – holding them submerged in the bath for what seemed an endless time, waiting for the fine strings of diamond bubbles to cease trickling upward from their pink nostrils, knowing their sleepless pink eyelids would never wake upon the world, waiting for their bodies to stop throbbing and go limp, was the worst thing I have done in my life. Some men, I suppose would have enjoyed it; but not me. And that's what Rudekamp meant when he called me weak – unable to relish life on its given terms. So be it. It's too late to try and change my character now.

But you, Doris, though in all the palaver of puppy-management you didn't even notice the two had gone missing, I've always wanted to clear this up with you: in a word, to say sorry. Not that it isn't too late for that as well. But some things have to be said because until they are said we will live, or will have lived, in false worlds. We did a Robespierre on you, severing the natural order for your greater good. But then what is natural and what is not? I think it was around that time that I started brooding on such things. That, anyhow, is what I've been trying to work my way around to with this letter.

And that's more or less all. I'll never become Head Boy now; but it wasn't on the cards anyway. As you see, I've made it into my last doglife. And that's finality of another measure; though if one of the merits of the doglife system is that one may actually enjoy the companionship of five successive dogs and learn to bestow one's love upon them, then I have failed on that as on so many other counts. Still, don't misunderstand me. Much as I valued your affection, I would never be so foolish as to take that as any sort of a testimonial to my character or moral worth. I know dogs are quite undiscriminating in such matters. That, of course, is the up-side of the rule of hierarchy.

But mentioning Rudekamp has reminded me of something I'd forgotten about that last conversation we had. At some point, when he'd come to a pause in his generally unremitting tirade about life and all things thereunto appertaining, I thought to ask how the kaffir – as he'd called him – had reacted to having the gun barrel slammed across his fingers. "Funny thing," he said. "He didn't react at all. It was amazing. I wouldn't even say that he blinked." He gazed into the distance for a few seconds, then added, "God, if only I had such strength..."

Rudekamp confessing to weakness? He didn't finish the sentence; and I wonder now what he was about to say, almost as if it had been one of those moments poised on the cusp of history like the moment a dog first licked a human's hand, or the moment a human first sang a two-note interval. Would he have said, "...I'd have beaten the lot of you from here to High Holborn."? Or would he, if he'd had the courage, or the honesty, have said something more unpredictable, more surprising?

I'll never know. But so long as such a question remains unanswered...

In Chrysalis

Railings. I'm walking past these railings, markings on an endless ruler – they do go on and on, longer than you'd expect, and I can't believe I'll ever again in the future think back on my schooldays without thinking of these railings painted brown, cast iron, going on and on and on. And then foot leather striking boards as I push through the door under the turret where the clock face is, and hear at once the feet of all the other girls hurrying, funnelling in, just in time, endless clumping of swing doors, and I take a deep breath of disinfectant-swabbed dust. These, I suddenly think, seem to have been the things that first spelled 'secondary school' to me, even though for the first three years one wasn't allowed to use the main door: the booming clatter; all scrubbed clean. When I was smaller I used to run my hand along those railings: not counting them – I've still no idea how many there are – but somehow taking account of them. Miss Poynter acknowledges me as we pass in the thronged corridor, and I smile as naturally as I can.

The fumes of mashed potato get everywhere – steam and hot aluminium – even up in the library where I'm spending a free period, then when the bell goes I'll go and eat my sandwiches in the shelter in the Spinney, all those unkempt rhododendrons with flowers the colour of a bishop's vest – though it's not the season for them now.

I'm scanning the shelves for books about the war, preferably with pictures, because Miss Poynter has set us a double homework to write either an essay or a story about it, and I've got an idea based on those scenes you see in films where soldiers are waiting around in railway stations, sitting sadly on their kit bags and smoking, so I want to do a story about a soldier going back to the front whose train is delayed for hours and who falls in love with the girl in the cigarette kiosk and they promise to write to each other. So I need to know things like whether soldiers always travelled in special trains, what their kit consisted of and how heavy it weighed, how often they got leave and what they were and weren't allowed to say in their letters home. Were cigarettes rationed? I could ask Daddy a lot of these things; but I want to show I can do a proper 'research'.

At the next table, some of the girls from my class are speculating as to what the subject will be for this year's 4th-form debate. Gillian Grange says she's prepared to bet it'll be Egypt – apparently Nasser has been up to a lot of strutting and swaggering during the holidays – and in fact she'll be proved right, but none of us know this yet and it probably hasn't even been decided. They're all saying it's unfair we have to have our debate in the first term of our year, which doesn't give us enough time; but of course the spring and summer terms always go to the 5th and 6th years. "Yes," says someone, "but we're the least experienced and we ought to get the most time..." I'm not really listening, though. I'm thinking about my only memory of the war, which is probably my earliest of all memories, when a great explosion makes the house shudder and a vase topples from the mantlepiece and Daddy dives forward and catches it like a fielder in a cricket match.

The partition walls are khaki with square high-up panes of pebbled glass, and the lights, which are also high, have dark green shades which have collected a lot of dust; and I start wondering whether I could use this for the design of the waiting room in the railway terminus in my story.

It's nearly time, and I go to put the books back in their places – not much help, and I'll have to try the reference library at the weekend – and I'm passing the table where Gertrude Burns and her friends are all of a huddle – Dirty Gertie, everyone calls her – and I see she's showing them something she's got concealed between the pages of a magazine; so I crane over to look, and she lets me see, and it's a picture of a man in his underpants. It's just an advertisement. But as the page turns I catch the glimmer of graphite, and I realise she's added some discreet shading to make it look as if his underpants are stretched with something very big inside them. The others snigger as I move sharply away.

Then, as I leave, I notice that the girls at the other table – the highbrows, who'd never be seen dead in Gertie's smutty circle – are glancing at me with that same look, that look I know so well, the look that says, 'Little Miss Prissy-boots...' I give them what I hope is a 'level stare'; and then the bell goes and I can make my exit with dignity.

So all the mounting rumours are confirmed. It's been announced in assembly that the subject of our end-of-term debate will be the political situation in Egypt with special reference to the Suez Canal. It's obvious I'm going to have to pay a lot more attention to the news, as everybody's saying the situation is already quite dangerous, and it'll probably go on developing right up to the day of the debate. That makes it very difficult. I haven't made up my mind whether to put my name down to speak. I'm terribly frightened of getting up with all eyes on me, and the lower school fidgetting and bored, and those of the 5th and 6th who deign to turn up – though of course they're all supposed to, but they don't – looking on with scorn and condescension. But I know that if I don't make myself do it this time, I'm all the more certain to funk it next year and the year after, when the standard is bound to get higher and higher.

At long last I get my story about the war back from Miss Poynter, and she has written "Very Imaginative" under it; so I proudly show it to my parents and leave it at home for them to read. Next evening, before dinner, I ask Daddy what he thought of it. Very methodically he opens his pen-knife and starts reamering out the bowl of his pipe with that horrible squealing noise that puts my teeth on edge; and he smiles the way he does when he's about to say something witty, and he says, "I liked everything about it except the story." Then he knocks out his pipe, and it strikes me that this sound – briar knocking against heavy cut glass – is something that has been repeating itself all my life like a judge calling the court to order or an auctioneer saying, "Going – going – ! – gone." Then Mum calls us in to dinner, and I'm very quiet because I'm trying to control my feelings; but afterwards, when we're washing up, I tell her what Daddy said: "I mean, it *is* a story, so if he liked every-thing but the story, he's saying he didn't like it at all, isn't he?" But Mum says he didn't mean it that way: "He told me he was quite impressed by your descriptions – daylight filtering in through the blacked-out roof of the station so that it looked like a cathedral – all that aspect of it..." Well, that mollifies me a little, especially since I worked that out for myself, what it must have looked like with the roofs all painted black but light beginning to leak in with the wear and tear. Even so, she hasn't got it quite right. I didn't say a cathedral, I said about the soldiers being knights going into battle and kneeling before an altar in a chapel to have their swords anointed. But then I say, "So what was wrong about the story, then?" and Mum says, "Oh, you know, just the business of the man-woman relationship. It's no criti-cism of your writing as such. You mustn't take it to heart. You can't be expected to understand – not just yet."

So it's that again! "You don't understand." Something they know and I don't. But they've obviously not the slight-est intention of explaining any of it to me. They won't even tell me what it is I fail to understand. "You'll realise later on." The understanding is presumably supposed to to pop into my head from nowhere, while they just wait on the sidelines and smile helplessly doting.

Unexpectedly, Hester invites me home to tea. I haven't had a proper friend since Jennifer and I quarrelled at the end of last term – I hoped it might be forgiven and forgotten once school began again, but she moves in a different circle now and speaks to me, *when* she speaks to me, as if I was someone behind the counter at the Post Office. I think of Hester generally as one of the highbrows, but she's quite kind all the same, and doesn't seem to mind talking to me.

There's rather a lot of furniture, and Hester and I sit with her parents around a low, round, copper-topped table. The china-ware is floral and old-fashioned, and the pastries have unusual things in them such as poppy seeds. Hester starts telling us all about a parody she's written in her head called 'The Teddy-Boys' Picnic', and she sings:

Ti-tum ti-tiddle-ti tum-ti-tum
You've reason to feel alarmed
Ti-tum ti-tiddle-ti tum-ti-tum
You'd better not go unarmed...

I don't remember the rest. When she's finished, her parents clap, so so do I, and her Dad gives her a smile that is more like a hug, and he glances at me and says, "Good sense of humour, my daughter!"

At one point, while Hester is out of the room, her father says to me, "Has it ever struck you that the start of *The Teddy-Bears' Picnic* is actually a variant on the *Dies Irae* plainchant?" I'm a bit bewildered; but he's not asking in the tone of a teacher wanting to test my knowledge, or of a parent trying to force a point of view onto me. I notice

Hester's mother's eyes twinkling mischievously, reassuringly, almost girlishly; and he goes on: "Obviously the infant who responds to the threatening quality of the tune can't possibly be making that connection. So what is it? Does it mean that there's something inherently sinister in that particular handful of intervals – some universality at work?"

When it's time to go home, Hester sees me to the door and I ask her whether she's going to put her name down to speak in the debate. She shakes her head with a downcast smile as if refusing some dish her doctor had advised her against; then she adds, "Anyway, Suez isn't the most important thing going on in the world." Well, I think, possibly it isn't, but it happens to be the topic we've been given, and not only that, it looks as if we're heading straight for another war, they're already sending planes from Cyprus to bomb the Canal Zone, and you can't say that isn't important. Again Hester gives me her sad old lady's smile, and I find myself wondering on the way home if she and her family are a special sort of people who are born old and then grow progressively younger.

It's not often I get the house to myself, and in fact until quite recently I've been nervous of being left alone. But for once my parents are off to the theatre with a business associate of Daddy's and his wife, and won't be back they say till nearly twelve. When I get home, there's a note on the table from Mum: "I've left some fishcakes under a cloth in the larder, and there are some boiled potatoes you can sauté up if you don't want to eat them cold. You can open a tin of garden peas if you like, empty the ones you don't use into a jar and cover them. Don't leave them in the tin, will you."

They've been saying there's going to be a special

announcement from the Prime Minister. I'd have liked to watch it on the television, but our tube has blown and Daddy says we can't afford a new one until the end of the month. I consider phoning Shirley to ask if her family will be watching – she only lives ten minutes away – but I decide not to bother, as I don't really fancy coming back to the empty house a second time because it's a bit spooky; so I listen on the radio instead. Sir Anthony Eden tells us how grave the situation is; and then Gaitskell comes on afterwards talking about a motion of no confidence. You'd think even the Labour Party would rally behind Britain at a time like this! I really ought to be making notes – get a special note-pad – even start clipping things out of the newspaper. Today I've taken my courage in both hands and put my name down to speak, but things have been happening so quickly in the last few days, and I realise I haven't kept pace with them, and there are four weeks to go in which all sorts can happen and I really haven't an iota of an idea what I want to say.

But that isn't the only thing I do that evening. In the little room that Daddy calls his study there's a glass-fronted book-case that he keeps locked. He only keeps it locked because the door swings open if you don't, and the key isn't really hidden, just dropped into a drawer of the bureau the book-case stands on; but nevertheless, there's still some suggestion of prohibition about a locked door. On the bottom shelf of the book-case there are some art books, and these have been tantalising me ever since Gertie showed me that picture, because it may be my chance to find out what men are really like. So I open the drawer I've never dared open before. Softly, softly, turn the key...

Raphael, Rembrandt, Van Gogh – they're heavy books, and I'm terrified of tearing the covers as I pull them out – nothing, not a single male nude except for the occasional baby Jesus, and I'm not looking for babies. Breughel – still nothing – Titian – ditto – Michelangelo... And there, a page turned like any other page, just as I'm about to give up: the answer to all my questions. I gaze at those little snail-curly appendages – not so different from a baby's as I'd imagined – and wonder whether the quickening of my pulse is not merely the consequence of the furtiveness of my actions, burglar in my own home. I dare myself to touch the statue of David – to touch him *there* – because that involves crossing some sort of mental barrier; but of course it's only paper. I even challenge myself with the idea of leaving the book open on Daddy's table, so that he'll know I know, and he will have to challenge me himself if he thinks I oughtn't to. But I do no such thing.

If I've achieved nothing else, though, I've at least settled the matter of Gertie's shadowed photograph. It was just her wild imagination.

Daddy gives me advice on how to deliver my speech: best not to write it down, because then you have to read it, and that doesn't look spontaneous enough because people tend to think what isn't spontaneous isn't sincere; and don't try to commit it to memory word for word, because then if you find you've forgotten a bit you'll be completely thrown and not know what to say next; use headings to glance at, preferably on an inconspicuous file card; you have to be clear what you're going to say – that goes without saying – but rely on your instinct once you've thought it through, and don't try to think it through in too much detail, trust yourself to fill in the gaps as they arise. I try to practise this technique in my bedroom, but only get into what Mummy would call a mugger's buddle; added to which, I'm really getting more and more confused about what I think about it. But I can't back out now.

In the school library, the highbrows are all looking terribly confident, sitting at their table by the window and saying things to each other like, "What is the difference between a war and a state of armed conflict?" and laughing together the way grown-ups do. Can you start by learning that laugh, I wonder, and build upon that, or do you have to have achieved some essential element of grown-upness first? And have I been more grown-up since I touched the picture of the 'David'? It seems not. Anyhow, I've decided to look into what lies behind the conflict over Suez, and I'm burrowing back into things like the Suez Canal Convention of 1888 and beginning to realise how much fun it can be to use indexes and bibliographies to trace your own path through the pages of different books and journals, almost like reading a book that doesn't exist except as a product of your activity.

I'm at Hester's for tea again, and her brother drops by, and she tells me he was in Egypt doing his National Service in 1953, before the troops were pulled out; so I decide the businesslike thing would be to ask him about it, but he just snorts and says the two worst aspects of Egypt were the flies and the women – in no particular order – then launches into a lurid description of bloated drowned dogs clogging the water-courses – the drinking water, that is – and of the smells, which brings him back again to the flies and the women; and there's a note of grievance about his way of telling me it, as if it was all my personal responsibility, or at least as if it was rude of me to have brought the subject up. Hester is embarrassed, and tells me afterwards to take no notice of him, and that it wasn't my fault, he's always like that when National Service is mentioned, she doesn't know why.

Back home I tell Mum and Dad what he said – though I miss out the part about the women – and how he seemed to think that was somehow a comment on the present situation; and then I add that of course it's all over now, isn't it, with the UNO sending in their police, and really the debate's going to be about history now rather than current events. But Daddy says he's not so sure it's over, and perhaps that's what my friend's brother was getting at, because it's pretty obvious the wogs won't be capable of running the canal. And then Mummy gives a smile with a slight puckering of the forehead, and Daddy gives a smile that says 'oops-a-daisy'; and I smile too because they are smiling. Then I find myself getting angry with myself for smiling, because I know what those smiles mean: they mean that 'wog' isn't a word you should call people, and it's all right for them to use it between themselves but not in front of me, and that it's not that it even matters whether I know the word – because after all, their smiles are embracing me – but that it shouldn't be done openly. Why am I smiling, then? Because I always do, always have done. Their smiles have always accompanied me, like the clonk of his pipe on the glass ashtray, smiles of approval that bear the threat of disapproval: yes – smile – that's the right way to stroke the cat – which means that the other way is wrong. All my life, they've been smiling me – yes, Miss Poynter, I do know that 'smile' is not a transitive verb – they've been smiling me into shape; and I have this vision of two people sharing an ice-cream cornet, taking alternate smooth licks at either side.

The hall echoing with the clatter of chairs being unstacked. Prefects bossing people about. Carafes of water on the speakers' table to give the proceedings an air of due seriousness. Teachers taking up their positions on the platform and along the side-aisles. Not packed out, but not a bad attendance either.

One by one the girls mount the steps to the platform, and they're talking about what America might do and what Russia might do, and who stands to gain what, and the maintenance of oil supplies and Israel's motives and Syria's interests, and how much is bluff, and their voices are terribly earnest and I realise I've been on the wrong track altogether. I've been swotting up on the Khedive Ismail – Disraeli bending Queen Victoria's ear behind parliament's back – and I've planned to begin, "In 1859, the governments of France and Turkey..." And my name is being called.

My legs nearly fail me as I go up the steps, and then I am saying, "Really this goes back to the 19th century. We took over control then – well, half control – because the Turks couldn't, and we've run things very well, Britain has run things very efficiently, all this time, and it's legally ours. The Company's, legally. You'll never get any respect in the world if you just let people have their own way, I mean if you don't stand up to aggression like we stood up in the last war..." – and I realise that's it. I've said all I meant to say, at least I've nothing left to say, and my speech is over. I return to my seat to a sprinkle of dutiful applause and some hollow, contemptuous laughter and sniggers.

But then, as luck will have it, I'm slightly let off, because Fats Willoughby is the next to speak, and she doesn't seem to have prepared anything at all, and perhaps she thinks she's replying to what I said, it's difficult to know: "You can't just say that because something happened in the past it's got to do with what we are now, who we are now. Just because we built it..." – she's obviously under the impression that Britain 'built', as she puts it, the Suez Canal – "it's ours as if we'd built it ourselves. Like Stonehenge. We didn't build that, because we're alive today, not then, and it's nothing for us to be proud about any more than we wrote Shakespeare's plays..." The giggles have been spreading fitfully almost from the moment she started, because people are always ready to laugh at anything Fats Willoughby says or does; but she battles bravely on, raising her voice so it starts to squeak: "We're told we mustn't blame the Germans today for what Hitler did, aren't we, so how can we say things like that and still try to take credit for what British people did all those years ago, and anyway there's plenty of bad things Britain's done, and we..." But by now waves of hilarity are sweeping through the hall, and Fats pauses for a second or two then gives up and comes down from the platform; and as she does so, she knocks a pile of papers off one of the tables, and we all laugh even more, because she's always knocking things over and everybody knows that.

The teachers, not laughing but nonetheless smiling, reassert their control and begin to calm the hall with soothing gestures; but I notice they don't attempt to do this until the uproar is already past its peak. They're skilfully riding the waves of the audience's feelings, their smiles sweeping back and forth across us like shoals of little sharp fish. As things settle down, I glance back to where Willoughby is sitting. We've both been given a tough time, and I feel a twinge of sympathy for her. Funnily enough, though, she seems quite calm and self-possessed, as if she feels she's made her point as best she can, and others can take it or leave it, and the fact that she's made herself look ridiculous is merely something thrown in, an extra included at no additional cost, all part of the service.

It's really too cold for sitting out in the shelter with my sandwiches, but I muffle up with my scarf and eat with my mittens on. I can't bear the looks. People are scarcely speaking to me now. Hester did smile across the classroom;

but she stayed with her own group. Even Fats Willoughby, who showed up worse than I did, has her friends – though they're rather silly friends.

Where are the secrets hidden? Or aren't there any secrets? I submit to being moulded by hints and smiles and things half said which can't be challenged or even recognised. What I'm doing when I return my parents' smiles is to accept that I Can't Be Expected to write a story about a soldier and a cigarette girl. Perhaps I can't be expected to understand the Suez situation either. Which is all very well, except that once you're up there on the platform, you're on your own; and you're expected to say something cogent and rivetting. Perhaps when I grow up I'll be a travel writer – just do the descriptions.

While I'm thinking all this, someone arrives and sits beside me. It's Dirty Gertie. She's never bothered who she speaks to. She reaches into her satchel and produces a greasy hamburger – must have sneaked out to the Wimpey Bar for it.

For a while we discuss the drizzle, and thank God term's nearly over. Then, after a pause and a mouthful, she says, "Do you play with yourself?"

"You mean solitaire – patience...?"

She looks at me until my cheeks begin to pink, then goes on: "You ought to. You're a big girl now. Adults all do it, even though they pretend they don't. My Auntie Gloria says a man's never enough; and even when he is, you shouldn't let yourself get reliant on them." She takes another bite out of her hamburger, then adds, "I bet your Mum does it."

That has me almost choking with anger and embarrassment, and I want to get up and leave, but I don't feel I can just walk away when she can see I haven't finished my packed lunch. Gertie, seemingly oblivious of my feelings, looks at me searchingly and then says, "Would you like me to show you how?"

I can't form a solitary word. The truth is – though I don't recognise this till later – I am half tempted. But then I become aware of the greedy look in her eyes; and I don't like greediness. I shake my head mutely, disengage from her gaze and settle to grimly chewing the rest of my sandwich while Gertie, seemingly unoffended and unconcerned, begins talking about next term's athletics.

'Prig.' That's the word they use about me. I don't often hear it spoken, but I know the looks that go with it. I've become sensitised to them.

I let it be known when I think something's not right. Is that bad? If you asked them, they'd say no. But behind your back it's a different story.

Yet you're supposed to stand up for what you believe in, aren't you? That's generally agreed. It's even considered admirable in many circumstances. Or in some people.

Perhaps the best thing is to be like Fats Willoughby: say your piece, let them like it or lump it, not mind if everybody jeers, even learn to derive self-respect from their jeering. But it's easy enough to look at things that way here in the comfort and dark of my bed. Even just switch on the light, and the world is an altogether different, colder place.

It's all supposed to come out right in the end, isn't it – the smiles and the things half said; and then all of a sudden I'll be there, a real me, out of the chrysalis, resplendent, refulgent, and all I'll remember of school will be the smell of swabbed grime engrained in floorboards, for which I'll feel a certain tenderness; and then one day a man will choose me – or I may even choose him, if he'll let me – and... I blush in the dark as the monstrous thought comes back, what Gertie said about Mummy; and just as a way of coping with it I try to force myself to imagine it, but the image won't form; and I try to think of her opening the book when she's alone in the house and looking at the photo of Michelangelo's David casually showing himself; but still my mind shrinks away and all I see is my mother's smile.

And I lie there, sleepless, wondering when I shall be free to smile my own smile with my own grubby secrets snug inside it.

Slug Heaven

ONE

In front of the unlit house, black slugs and brown slugs cruised the slate wastes of the flagstones. Their periscopes peered through the atmosphere's invisible strata to where the great numinous slug-trail of the Milky Way glimmered from horizon to horizon to bless their base endeavours. As modelled by their intelligences, the upper spaces were composed of a substance not unlike the secretions of their own glands, this being squeezed at levels of particularly high pressure until droplets formed as if in a tight fist. Such bands of variation in pressure, occurring at more or less regular intervals, formed a system of striations constituting a kind of cerebral ladder which dripped like the ledges of a waterfall and which linked their lowly selves to the divinity often, as now, manifesting itself in full and eerie splendour. On her arrival, Petra would notice that the shallow undulations of the stone terrace were slicked with a treacherous slipperiness through which twinkling, criss-cross wakes echoed the firmament.

Slugs. Have to do something about them if I want to grow lettuces. Broken-up egg-shells – that's supposed to stop them, I remember. In an old Kenco jar; that guy who used to fill jars with queasy objects. What was his name? Sometimes they were only rubber bands, different thicknesses, looked like pickled guts. Need to eat a lot of eggs, though. They can't slide over them, I assume. Still, there aren't likely to be any lettuces now – must go up in daylight; see what's left, if anything. Where's the damn keyhole? They did say the kitchen door, didn't they? Stiff, stiff... there... Jesus, it's cold!

Standing in the middle of the living room she dropped the valise she had lugged the final half-mile from the bus-stop: intruder in a fortress whose garrison had absconded and were unlikely ever to return. The place was called Bryn Derwen; but she had seen no sign of oaks, only the ivy-hugged larches tilted over the lane, water-sodden, ready to topple. She felt the chill of the stone floor rising through the soles of her shoes – felt it making her bones stiff and brittle – as, by the ceiling light in its dust-fluffed woollen shade, she surveyed the bound boxes and the two chairs and the wrapped rolls of materials and the oddments scattered on the trestle table and concluded that, so far as she could tell, everything was present. But there was a wrong feel about it; and she realised it was that the room and its contents had the air of something long abandoned rather than of something newly arrived and awaiting a commencement.

At least they put up the trestle table. Generous to a fault. But the stove: what is it it reminds me of, all that ash spilling out? I know – cooled pumice. Pompeii. People cast from life, then burned out of the matrix – dispensable as lost wax... No coal in the scuttle. Assume some's been delivered – I paid for it. But I'm not going out again to the shed now. Just settle for a packet soup and some toast; then a stiff Scotch, then bed. There was an electric fire somewhere, wasn't there? Under the stairs? It'll take an age to get any warmth into these walls.

Seated at the table, her feet raised onto a strut to avoid contact with the floor, she noticed the old biscuit tin embossed with the image of a highland piper and dragged it across and opened it to release into the sepulchral air the smell of childhood: plasticene. Yes, all those Christmases, once the family had got it into their heads that she had the aptitude, without fail: presents of barbola paste, glitter wax and, above all, slim Pan-pipes of plasticene in toytown tints which would eventually become aggregated into a subtle polychrome bolus like a monster marble or giant's gobstopper – flecks of dusky crimson, clouds of navy, whorls of mustard – before finally settling into a uniform, hippopotamus grey-brown which she'd learned to find companionable. Lifting the fused mass, she tried to tear off fragments; but it was far too hard. Finally she gripped a knobble and twisted it as if wringing the neck of a fowl until it parted, leaving at each side a wrenched spiral. She pressed and squeezed it between palms warmed by her soup mug until, after a long time, it became malleable.

There's a resilience, elasticity, which I missed at first when I started working with clay without quite knowing what it was I was missing. Clay just sits there; but this stuff reacts. Take some away, and you've got to re-shape what's left. Pinch it here and there. Roll it into the general form. Podgy fingers – but no, not quite, more sleek than that. Even elegant. And their heads are almost cubic, aren't they, little boxes. And the eyes are on very fine stalks – have to cheat a bit there. And at the rear end, two little prongs pointing upwards – is that right? It looks right. What else? Ah yes, the horizontal ribbing of the body, or of the last two thirds of the body – like macaroni – rake those out with a blunt pencil – as if to aid air-flow, lend speed, or to stabilise their passage, stop them rolling in an aqueous environment; but they don't live in an aqueous environment. Oh, and I'd forgotten, there's that little oval hole in the neck where they probably breathe; and inside that you can see a sort of filigree fleshy lattice. May even be their lungs. Need my fine spatula for this; but it's in one of those crates somewhere. The clip on the cap of a Bic – that'll do...

So how long will it take me to collect enough egg shells? Mum used to say you could dissolve them with salt – just sprinkle salt on them, and they'd turn to water. Hideous thought, all your internal organs deliquescing while you writhed and struggled... I couldn't... Sifta salt used to have that picture on their canisters. Oh no, actually that was something else. A chick. A boy sprinkling... one of those pointless Victorian jokes: 'How do you catch a chicken? – Sprinkle salt on its tail.' Saw in the paper not so long ago that in some Chinese zoo – Shanghai, perhaps – there are stalls where visitors can buy live chicks to toss to the alligators...

She slammed her fist down onto the table. She trembled violently for a moment or two, a tree shaken by an unexpected gust, then drew herself up straight and sat there mute as a statue, taking long, deep, regular breaths. She sat like that for several minutes.

I was going to order a paper – every other day, I thought, or perhaps just once a week – but I won't. I just can't bear it any more. I don't want to see what's in the paper. I'll just listen to the news on the radio now and then, just to keep up. Or perhaps not even that. It's not as if my knowing what's going on could make a scrap of difference. Better stay here with what I've got, and limit myself to that. Like the plasticene: a dented putty-ball of dun mud, which is all that's left of the multifarious impressions and delights of childhood. I notice that when I move my slug there's a greasy patch. Must be paraffin-based to judge by the smell. I wonder if you could use that on paper to inhibit an India-ink wash? Perhaps get a fresh graphic effect that way. They have a sort of fringe around the bottom of their skirts, don't they? Leave it overnight on a leaf from a pad of drawing paper.

Why didn't I guess – damp bed-linen! Obviously hasn't been aired for months. Not that there's much I could have done about it without the stove. One of these blankets seems OK; but it's going to mean sleeping fully dressed tonight. No use trying to find an alternative. There isn't one. Just have to hope the mattress and pillow don't start oozing moisture when my body-heat gets to them.

★

Disassemble the newspaper. Take one double-page at a time, crease it along the diagonal and fold it into a long, loose strip about one-and-a-half inches wide; then bend this strip into a loop and coil the ends around each other leaving a short length protruding as a sort of touch-paper. That's how I was taught to make fire-lighters as a kid. I dare say you could simply scrunch the paper up and it would do the job; but I like to do it properly. I get a satisfaction from the continuity, even though I haven't needed to lay a fire for years – decades. Odd that the continuity of an action should comfort you long after you've stopped thinking very often about your parents. It's the newspaper I bought to read on the train. Didn't finish the crossword.

I feel a bit of a slag, having slept in my clothes; but the weather's clear, and it's good to be able to start getting things organised. The sheets are out on the line, snapping in the breeze. The shed's too leaky for the bike – it'll have to be consigned to the spare bedroom; but there's a sturdy wooden box – looks as if chicken feed's been kept in it – that'll do for a clay bin. And there's an old pram in there too that'll be useful for the shopping, as I think the terrain's going to prove too hilly for heavily-laden cycle trips. The wheels are a bit stiff, but I noticed a half-empty jar of Vick in the bathroom cupboard; I'll grease them with that... Briefly I visualise the spectacle of myself: a dotty old woman striding out, grieving for the unconceived. But I reject it. Stout cord trousers and an abb sweater.

I knew there'd be something missing – there always is. It's the anglepoise. I'll have to shift the table closer to the little window, and otherwise do the best I can with one of the bedside lamps from upstairs. The front door doesn't open. No key to be found. The little room which would be to your right if you did come in through the front door – the one under the spare bedroom, that is – will be sufficient for all the boxes, stands, materials, the short zinc bath for plaster: anything I'm not using at any particular time: a stores, in a word. As my kitchen utensils occupy only a few hooks, one shelf and a plate rack, the drawers under the sink can accommodate my points, mallets, claws, files, wire-cutters... The place is beginning to feel as I'd hoped: dedicated to its purpose as a trawler or a mine-sweeper.

The kitchen garden, on a steep slope behind the house, is almost choked with bramble which has come down in great hoops, great arching strands from the thicket above to take root where they touch and make that the bridgehead for further waves of encroachment. There's something almost malign about it: purposive yet mindless, blind yet inexorable: as if such advance could never be stopped; as if civilisation must eventually fall to it. I'll have to take serious action. And provender? Not much sign, though you can see where onions and lettuces may have been. There's a goose-berry bush savage as a Grunewald crown of thorns, and one or two up-ended bottomless zinc buckets presumably once used for forcing rhubarb. Prodding with a wobbly fork unearths a handful of potatoes, perhaps still edible, a trophy of sorts. You can look in, from here, through the tiny window on the landing of the staircase; but it makes me oddly uneasy. Back on the terrace, on the lee side of the house, I discover that a bramble has looped right down to the paving and, finding the darkness under a black plastic bag of rubbish, has begun to make a root where there's no soil to accommodate it. I pull out the strand and examine this deathly pale starfish, each of whose probing fingers has other stumpy growths beginning to sprout from it, and suddenly I realise what it is making me think of: the splash of Gilmour's semen when he used to come inside me. With a disgust I am at once ashamed of feeling, I drop the thing. The light is failing. Time to return indoors.

She spent that evening drawing slugs. She tried some experiments with wax pencil, but threw them away. Next day she mixed some plaster in a bowl, cut some chicken-wire roughly to shape as a stiffener, and modelled a group of fractal starfish which she mentally dubbed 'semen-stars'. It was raining heavily. She seemed a prey to indecision, walking from room to room. During a break in the down-pour she went out to look at the sky. It was blackly grey as an open-cast coalmine scarred with the teeth of gigantic chain-buckets, and the thunder was the thunder of machin-ery, never falling silent yet never quite spending its rage.

I know myself. Or at least, if I don't by now...When I'm not sure how to proceed, I tinker with method. Plasticene-stained paper – none too promising. Slugs and semen-stars? Who knows – you have to work around an idea; and if you don't know where the idea is, you have to work at random, or at what seems like random, or at whim, until you discover what it is you're working around. All right, I know the subject; but a subject's nothing without an approach. No, don't be offended; I know what I'm talking about. Or if I don't by now... I shan't abandon you – or rather, I shall not abandon the attempt to find you. Trust me – even though I am not entirely sure I can trust myself. I have no choice.

I don't much care for looking at my past work. Even if it had any merit, it's too late now for me to benefit. I've taken other routes. But this pad has sketches of Tina when she was pregnant, huge in the hammock, telluric tummy, a swollen fruit, the sketches that eventually led to those hammock sculptures which mutated in time into seed-pods swinging by hooks and chains. Gilmour and the others started calling it my 'organo-symbolic' period, which was almost enough to make me abandon it. Can't someone develop a visual language without its being categorised as a 'period'? Did anyone before Picasso have 'periods'? Wasn't one just expected to grow and mature? Well, anyhow... There are also some studies here – early ones – for what was to become my Buchenwald series, which I rather kept to myself. Began with my sketches from photographs of young women – images from ads – and wondering were they sylph-like or were they anorexic or were they maltreated, and how you'd register the difference; reading around the subject, learning; ligaments and wasted muscles like straps of iron, like twisted wire; and over and over, attacking the paper with a hard pencil, scratching it, scuffing it, trying to build up dark marks from a 4H as if even this small and innocent area of the cosmos must be forced to bear the scars of suffering – or, as we'd have been more likely to phrase it in those days, exhibit the evidence of struggle. But no, I more or less kept them to myself. Wasn't sure I had the right.

All that condensation – can't all be from my breath, can it? A strange effect, almost lithographic, those grey smears of atomised moisture with the darkness behind them. A chunky angel – could be Barlach; and on the other pane a profile, just sketched in a series of sweeps, with an expression I can't interpret and almost certainly couldn't have invented. Yet all with my breath. My breath and my sweat. But where do the forms come from? Old unnoticed wipings with grimy dishrags. Would there be, I wonder, a way to preserve them? Photosensitive paper, perhaps. You'd have to expose it on the dry side – out-doors, against the light. Then, of course, you'd see it in negative; but the photosensitive paper would reverse that again. A quick dip in hypo, or whatever it's called. I've no idea if that would be possible, but it might. It's going to rot the transoms of the window-frame, though, all that moisture – my moisture. My very substance rots my habitat – even as I try and manipulate other substances into new configurations. Constant interchange.

At least it's not raining this morning. I dreamt last night about the brambles. But oddly enough it wasn't a threatening dream, because the hooped succession of their progress brought to mind something from my early teens, when it was still the done thing to 'go for a drive' at weekends: the old Morris 8, sit-up-and-beg job, I think it was pre-war, with its ribbed leather seats and its trafficators that squeaked with the strain on their solenoids and its kicky crank-handle and its trouble with steep hills. We came to Welwyn late one afternoon, September or October, the light already declining, and found ourselves gazing up at the great viaduct – simple, repetitive, geometrical but cyclopean – its arches striding across the utterly silent valley; and I couldn't say then – and I doubt that I could honestly say now – just what it was about that scene that inspired me with such a sense of timelessness, of the benevolence of life. The stately marshalling of absence, possibly? Now, though, the hoops of bramble threaten to engulf me with their recursive energies. I'm reminded of the story once told me by a Polish count who was chatting me up at a private view. After the defeat of their armies in 1939, he said, the remnants of the Government had crossed the border into Romania, which was at that time a friendly power with whom they had a treaty. There they were put up in an exclusive luxury hotel. Unfortunately, there was a coup in the middle of the night in which a pro-Nazi party took over. The Poles woke up to find that the hotel had been surrounded by barbed wire. It had become a prison.

So fairy tales do come true! Drinking my coffee in the kitchen, I can look out through the glass pane of the door and see the distant ridges where the larches comb the mist as if carding wool. I must explore those paths one day. But not until I've got some real work done.

She set to work with every appearance of confidence. Choosing a firm wooden pallet about eighteen inches square, she nailed onto the centre, from below, a ten-inch upright of two-by-two. Then she retrieved from one of her boxes a tangle of lead-sheathed electrical wiring – not easy to come by, but she had found it on a skip – which she proceeded to staple to the top of the upright, thus forming an armature. For a few moments she looked at this structure as if dissatisfied with its proportions – or perhaps entertaining the possibility that the work might already be finished, that the twisted thicket of wires told all that needed to be told of the person whose portrait this was intended to be, and whose grubby little news photos were scattered there on the table. Then she reached into the bin and brought out a dollop of clay which she slammed down on the table and began kneading and slapping into a uniform consistency before squeezing it lump by lump into the gaps between the wires. Soon the wires were scarcely visible. The wooden upright was totally encased, and the thing had begun to take on a certain totemic and rude resemblance to a human neck and head: a sort of ovoid poised upon a pillar. At this point, however, she seemed to lose momentum. She sat down in an attitude of broken slackness and considered what she had done.

Bloody chaff's ripping my hands. Serves me right for being too impatient to swill out the bin first. But I do rather like the texture it gives it. Maybe I should save this batch for the outer surface. But where am I going – that's the point. Would I be better off working straight in plaster? Or both at once, turn and turn about? No, it's not that. The problem is, I'm jumping the gun. I'm not ready for this stage yet. It needs another form of exploration first, another form of address.

What form of address, then? What exactly is the question I can't quite bring to the surface of my mind, because my mind's perhaps too focused on you and not enough on the materials despite my preliminary efforts, my attempts to limber up? Is that what it's about? And if that is what it's about, then how does the problem express itself as a problem? I mean, in what guise? In what guise is the root problem manifested as a working difficulty? It's something to do with the relation of the two-dimensional to the three-dimensional. Not the geometrical relation – I know all about that – but the... I can't come up with the terminology; but first there was you, with a certain bone-structure and certain choices of personal grooming and certain experiences etched in your flesh regardless; then there are these photographs, none easily legible, no two appearing to represent the same person but nevertheless all genuine; and then there's what I am trying to... What is it that slab of clay reminds me of with its ridges, its almost landscaped ridges?

All at once she rose and went into the kitchen where there hung behind the door a stiff, greasy, dun coat, locked into its shape, unwearable. She returned to her work-room, hung the coat on a hook and began to draw it in a large-format Daler sketch book. She drew it boldly, filling the page, imparting to the soiled and mildewed material a monumental dignity. Then, with every appearance of irritation, she unhooked the coat and lay it flat on the table and began drawing it again. She could, one supposes, simply have turned her original page on its side; but the difference must in some way have been important to her.

It's like bronze – neglected bronze, dulled by the elements. That streak of mildew could almost be an efflorescence of copper oxide. It holds its shape, immobile. You can draw it as if it were thrown over the body of a fallen soldier, stiffened with his soaked blood. Yet what I have on the page is neither bronze nor cloth, but a sort of dematerialisation poised like a spectre between the two: a space for thought. Now I understand. Tomorrow I'll start in earnest.

Growling and rattling, the post van bumped up the lane bearing nothing but a telephone bill. She took no notice. She was setting the sails for some journey of the spirit. Clearing a space on the trestle, she rolled out a stretch of three-foot-wide cartridge paper, turned the roll back on itself and ripped along the crease with a steel rule, making a raw but straight edge. Standing on a chair, she tacked this to the wall. She did that three times; and the room brightened as if the sails had taken light from some unfathomable source to billow forth in a perverse purity. Next she went into the store room and rummaged in a black canvas satchel, from which she retrieved a folder, and drew from a cardboard cylinder a large sheet of brown wrapping paper. This she laid flat on the table. The folder contained pages of A4 – sixteen in all – which had been blown up on a photocopier from a single photograph in a book; and these she arranged on the brown paper until she had them in the right order and properly aligned. Then, one by one, with paste from a viper-hissing aerosol, she gummed them into place and fixed the assemblage alongside the white sheets; and she stood back and looked at it: a puffy, blotched face with Fu Manchu eyes and with dark patches where shadows would not have been.

Lesions, contusions, scratches, grazes, weals – a lexicon of affront. Jesus, the pigs really worked you over, didn't they. And then, for reasons known only to themselves, they took a photograph of their handiwork. But what did you really look like? That's what I want to find out. No two pictures alike; and some of them so small I can't even be sure whether you're wearing glasses or not; some of them with that curious tartan effect that comes of making a plate from a previous news-photo. Did you use make-up – I mean, obviously they wouldn't have let you – but before? I doubt it. You had your pride. And your hair? Is that a prison hair-cut, rough and ready, the work of an unskilled trusty, designed to humiliate; or is it the image you chose to project, a defiance, a rejection of something?

Tracing paper. Roll it out, crease it firmly with the thumbnail then lift the roll, pull at exactly the right angle, and a clean tear straight along the line. That's something I learned to do at the drawing office. Really impressed the juniors. They'd try it for themselves and rip the sheet in half... Experience counts. That's what it was meant to say. So, now: clip this over the collage... Do you see? Slowly, mark by mark, taking plenty of time to think about it, I'm going to reverse the process: draw you as you were before they did it: draw you without those awful marks, or perhaps first draw them then rub them out. A work of subtraction. At the same time, on these blank sheets, I shall perform a work of addition: build up my knowledge line by line, let them learn from each other. Some of those minor cubists – Gleizes, Metzinger – the less wild and wilful ones. A line. Flat carpenter's pencil. A line that traces the light on one side of your head. And all at once the shamanic magic is evident: the map of the spirit journey begun.

The forest path's been churned by half-tracks, the ruts are full of debris, of pine splinters. I've scarcely climbed above the level of the house, but already I'm enveloped in a fine grey mist that seems not to swirl but just to hang here. No fear of losing my way. There seem to be no forks in the path. A grey silk curtain behind which you could almost think there was nothing.

It reminds me of the day I came. Fog for the entire journey, or at least the first four hours of it, rubbing against the train's filthy windows, nothing to see but piles of discarded sleepers and the occasional machine-ripped hedgerow close to the line or the occasional burnt-out carriage in a siding. Then, when we were nearly here, I shook myself out of a stupor to realise that the lights of a town were twinkling in the distance. By then, of course, it was pitch dark. And it all seemed somehow appropriate. A complete interregnum. A passage through nothingness from one something to another something, a something not yet known.

A huge brown slug – must be all of eight inches long. It isn't moving. Maybe it's dead. Old and leathery, with what seem like scars on its back. I suppose they must, in time. Normally they're encased in a film of mucus which probably conceals the scars, just as a film of rain conceals the scratches on a car's paintwork made by the milled edge of a coin in the hand of a vindictive policeman.

The fog was a succession of dismal cupboards opening only on further cupboards. But she persisted. She followed the path up its irregular incline until the air grew lighter – perhaps an indication that trees had been cut from the flanking slopes – until, after about half an hour, she reached what seemed like a circular arena almost with the dimensions of a temple and the ambience of a sacred clearing, though in fact it was probably only a place for heavy logging plant to turn around for the journey back. She stood in the centre of this strange space; and at just that moment the fog began to lift; and as it lifted, it revealed a stricken landscape in which the silhouettes of a few trees, snapped as if by shell-fire, tilted at sharp angles. What seemed at first to be rank and file of tombstones, bone-white, were revealed as the mist dissipated to be bark-stripped pale stumps left by the chainsaws. Water dribbled aimlessly through the rot-brown underbrush to soak into the scree which floored the area. It was a place where one's eyes were drawn mercilessly to seek out a torn tunic, a tin hat star-scarred and rusting, a severed and rat-gnawed arm. And there above, against a blue the colour of Basildon Bond notepaper, hung, as if from a rafter, the lifeless flitch of the half moon.

I guess that's where it began, isn't it – I mean really began – in the Great War: the mechanisation of death. And of life, for that matter. Passing above the house before the little lane that descends to it, I spot a collapsed wooden structure underneath a mass of briar. It's an old outdoor privy. And probably not so very old, at that. It's not so long since human beings had to bury their own dung like animals. And it's only a matter of time before these woods will be privatised – it's happening already in some parts – and we'll be forbidden to walk in them; and in the fields, on the lower slopes, genetically engineered sheep will be cropping genetically engineered grass, and they'll be surrounded by high steel fences and razor wire so that not a seed can be purloined by a rival enterprise to infringe the patent – no, not even by the wind. It's a narrow band of history we've got, to inhabit the countryside, to find retreat in it. From here I can almost see down my own chimneys. Soot. That's a thought. I could map your bruises in soot, apply it with my thumb: not the face, just the bruises. I wonder if fixative would stabilise soot; or would it smear it, make it greasy?

★

Keith Jarrett on the cassette player – a long, long, solo improvisation that seems to become becalmed for minutes on end before setting off on another train of reasoning, never quite dying, always new options opening up, given time... Sit still in my mind while I draw you. Or a version of you, a possible you, a visitation.

A far cry from the drawing office, that's for sure. Twenty years I was there. Twenty very long years. They called us lady tracers. Men didn't do that job; or if they did, they were called junior draughtsmen. We used to joke that we'd be better off as Lady Dockers. It was my parents' idea. Everyone agreed that I had 'artistic leanings', and that seemed the best outlet for my talents that would also enable me to make a living. From there, it was suggested, I could eventually find an opening in commercial art and in time, perhaps – it was not impossible – find some way of fulfilling my 'ambitions'. So that's how I ended up in structural engineering. It wasn't my parents' fault. They had no better idea than I did – let alone the careers guidance people. And anyhow, there probably wasn't much of an alternative for someone of my background, not in those days. But I did become head of the department, which by that time had developed into quite a big department, so I managed to save up my pennies and eventually decided to take the plunge and sign on for an extension course in the fine arts. That's where I met Gilmour and the gang. We were all mature students, although I was close to being the maturest – joke – I mean the oldest – but we took the business of being students terribly seriously; did it properly: the endless late-night discussions in bare-boarded squats where someone would keep up an endless supply of lethal Turkish coffee from one of those copper things – pans – hardly the shape to be called pans, somehow – with a long brass handle...

Think of the body-work of a car. When it's new and unscathed, there's something about the gloss – the continuity, perhaps it is – the gloss of the spray-painted surface that makes it look almost solid, invulnerable. But the moment the car's had the slightest bump, the surface dents; the paint flakes off and rust encroaches; and the whole thing is revealed as weak, tinny, nothing more than a skin. Now look at this drawing. You see? It's the same with human flesh. You don't realise so long as it's undamaged. The face assumes the scrutability of an icon. But once it's cut, bruised, scabbed, it congregates uncertainties: Who is this really? What's under her surface? What was her value?

Mad about cars, weren't you, you lot. I think of you all in a Cadillac the size of Cleopatra's barge, clapped out, falling to pieces – stolen, inevitably – psychedelically decorated with flames from the engine and a spray of fake bullet-holes as an up-yours to the police, the bonnet springing open at every traffic light so that one of you has to rush out and slam it shut again. Puts me in mind of that Godard movie – *Bande à part...*

Look, what the fuck did you really think you were doing?

Oh well...

I was taken up by a gallery once, for a while – would you believe that? Very comfortable. 'Bourgeois' is the word you'd have used, though as a matter of fact that word isn't used so much these days – at least, not as a term of all-purpose denigration. Anyhow, it didn't last long. I always bristled when they referred to my work as the 'product', and even more so when they started talking about quality control. Young people – a new attitude. It all came to a head when I started working in a style they said the collectors wouldn't associate with me – though for me it hadn't been all that radical a departure. They came on heavy with, "We've invested a great deal in promoting your work, blah-blah-blah..." – virtually accusing me of commercial malpractice for wanting to develop in the way that seemed to me perfectly logical. So that was that. I told them to stuff their contract. Meant I never got a penny for the pieces they managed to sell after I'd waltzed off, of course.

That was when a group of us, all former student friends, got together to launch the 'flying exhibition' tactic. We called it that after the 'flying universities' in the Eastern bloc. We'd set up our work just for a day or so in places we'd broken into: derelict greengrocers' with flyposted windows, discontinued public conveniences with the fittings ripped out, narrow buildings where rusty jibs with cast-iron pulleys still hung hinged over roller-shutter frontages, hulks too silt-bound to rise with the tides... The trick was to make sure all the right people knew it was happening, then vacate the premises before anyone could take action. Sundays were a good time for it.

All the same, when you take yourself out of the system that assigns the values which society as a whole accepts, you're left in a no-man's land, a place without stars or compass. There'd been a temporary intersection between my own inner pilgrimage and the meandering path of public taste – which is to say, fashion. Could one honestly say that counted for anything? Yet without it there was no triangulation with the real world.

So what proof do I have that my work's any good? You've a right to know, after all. The only answer I can give is: just my own conviction and the faltering esteem of friends. But to you, at least, that shouldn't sound unfamiliar.

Yes, one forgets. There used to be alternative pathways through society – a little soggy underfoot, perhaps – alleys where people would meet in small groups and clusters and speak – speak in whispers even though the thought-police never ventured there – burrows where talent could fester and re-infect itself. Now life is lived more and more under the searchlight and the eye of the CCTV camera... But you had more than your share of that, too.

Christ, I'd forgotten just how frightful they are, these prison mug-shots! So flat, so soot-and-whitewash – as if your face had been blasted, pressure-hosed with light, light from the camera's direction, a twelve-bore discharge forcing the head back, flattening it against that tile wall where the hair and the shadows splash out black as blood – your blood – and the look of astonishment. You held up banks like a troupe of clowns, yet here in this Medusa image with the muscles of your throat so tightened that the thyroid and cricoid cartileges are thrust into prominence there's a look of mingled disbelief and resentment, plus perhaps a residual defiance, a very residual defiance, as you find yourself smashed into your own shadow by the force of their brutal arcs. What can I do with these images – how deconstruct them, reverse their time's arrow, reverse the blame, reverse the decisions that led you to it? They remind me of images shot in a centrifuge, except that your face is pulled not downwards but back as if by the wind against which even the angel of history cannot prevail. Can I find any way, with my clay and my plaster and my childish plasticene, my bourgeois good will and my political rags and tatters, to rescue you from the two-dimensionality into which you've been hammered by that screaming volley of light? How they must have hated you!

Superciliary crest. Zygomatic bone. Canine fossa... I sometimes wish I could make sculpture simply by stroking the air – like making music on a thérémin, or like gently smoothing the hair out of one's eyes. But not really. We need the resistance. We need the world to engage in dialogue with us. Mind you, people who love objects, who like to touch things – even to touch people – are already being regarded in some quarters as Neanderthal precursors of humanity proper – humanity as freed into pure cerebration.

Jarrett holds the keys down and thumps the piano. Gets a haunted chord.

Here's something that would surprise you: there's no generation gap any more. Oh yes, I talked about those young men at the gallery – very much 1980s figures – and yes, they're a new and upcoming breed – or were. There'll always be new styles of behaviour. But the complete rejection of one generation by another, the blanket attribution of guilt to one's elders... No. Since the fall of communism, we've all been children. No-one's experience is any more useful than anyone else's. None of us, if we're honest about it, knows anything. You should have seen the pundits and the commentators, the experts and the political theorists – not to mention the lecturers in cultural studies. Like beached fish, they were: grotesque, carbuncled and gulping. Their mouths still opened and closed from force of habit; but no sound came out – not, that is, until the tide of another discourse rose around them and gradually, spluttering a bit, they got back into the swim of things and resumed spouting their certainties without for a moment admitting they weren't exactly the same certainties as before. But no-one truly knows what the world is about nowadays. Everything's reduced to the compass of the personal, even the daydream.

The thing about Jarrett is that he shares his time with us. I know, I know: you could say that about any musician you hear on a record; and strictly speaking you'd be right. But there's something about the way Jarrett plays that makes you aware of his life passing as yours passes listening to him. You proceed at the same pace. He hasn't just thrown it off and left you to make what you will of it. He stays with you, he sees you through it.

How did you feel, I wonder, when someone stroked your cheek lightly with the back of his fingers or brushed the hair out of your eyes? Actually I know the answer. It made you feel cheap – bourgeois – the perfect little hausfrau. Eh? It's all right, I'm not being critical. I know you paid – paid with your life... Wait a minute: paid with your life for not liking your husband to stroke your cheek? Well, it does rather seem like that at times. In the end, you wouldn't even speak to your children. There's a lot I still don't understand.

An assumption I have never questioned, since it seemed self-evident, is that these shocking and demeaning snapshots did not conform to your own self-image, were not the image you would have wished to represent to the world. Yet in a sense that is exactly what they were, since you acted in such a way as to bring them about, created the circumstances where these images would represent you to the exclusion of any others.

Every so often I have to stop. Does that surprise you? After all, to you things must have seemed quite obvious – self evident. The straight and narrow path of inevitability.

How much of Keith Jarrett's time has he shared with us?

And now, asleep, I dream of you.

You walk towards me through a clothing store, Carnaby Street fashions have swept Europe, PVC boots and microskirts flaunt our availability, and you think, 'Is this progress, this medley of body-odours as women try on dresses all elbowing in a dim cellar like slaves in a ship's hold?'

You walk towards me through a crowd who are still

applauding your speech, an ovation due to a diva whom their eyes clothe in silks and diadems and whose arms they would pile with bouquets of unseasonable blooms, turning their heads for a glimpse as you pass, and you think, 'What difference will this have made?'

You walk towards me through a toy-department where Santa sits in his grotto while cuddly flameproof green bunny rabbits mutate into green plastic combat fatigues and green plastic Armalites and you think, 'Is this the initiation of the individual; and if so, is it the only way possible?'

You walk towards me through the starless night wailing like Cassandra and calling upon the dark itself for final vindication of your prophecies – the absolute blackness. Faced with the self-authentication of the admirably wise, you had chosen doubt. Faced with the victory of the word, you had chosen silence. Or so it seems to me in my dream.

Look, I like this small study – India ink. Reminiscent of Marcoussis, perhaps – one of those who sought an underlying rationality, even a kinship with machine drawing. Slippage of planes. Every intersection a cicatrice: tastefully shaded.

Sometimes I draw a line on the paper and imagine that, because the line was prompted by a profound emotion, it must of necessity communicate that emotion to others. But it doesn't, does it? That's not how things work. So all that's there is the line, begging for sympathy – or at least a modicum of attention. Did you ever, struck by this thought, stop short in your progress towards Utopia, then wonder why you had stopped, only to find that the thought had already escaped you? 'Just what was it that seemed so important only a few moments ago?'

I am far away in time and space. My fingers are swollen with the cold. Help me.

★

One of our group, a rather quiet woman called Harriet, used to make what she called pebble pieces. You know how you can walk along a beach when the tide's ebbed, and your eye is caught by the most beautiful pebbles in lustrous colours which seem to resonate with the hues of the sky, and you pick up the ones that particularly appeal to you and you take them home; and then, when you see them dried out, without their coating of water, you find them terribly disappointing? Well, what Harriet used to do was set such pebbles on a bed of sand in a shallow box with a glass top – the sort of thing a child would keep hamsters in – and concealed underneath it there'd be a tank of water and a tiny pump fitted with a time-switch; and each one was arranged so that the water would rise twice a day to engulf the stones, then would sink again. Every piece was accompanied by a booklet of tide tables for the particular stretch of coast where the pebbles had been found. Objective: no more disappointment.

Most of the others were a bit sniffy about her work: thought it a trifle kitsch. But I liked the things – almost wish I'd bought one from her to have here and remind me that there are other places in the world, other truths, or other moments of truth. How can you judge? The quality of people's work, I mean. One of the men used to talk about his idea for a small box, a small box locked with a padlock, which would rattle softly and mysteriously when you picked it up – something like one of those marble mazes – and it would have a certificate of some sort with it saying that if the lid were ever opened, its value as art would be nullified. He used to call this his Schrödinger's Cat project; and the question was, he said, would the person who bought it open it? This was someone who never actually made the works he fantasised – which, in his view, would have bordered on vulgarity – but referred to them always as 'thought-pieces', on analogy with 'thought-experiments'.

I know what you'd have said about such matters – at least I think I do. You'd have said that the idea of comparative value in works of art is merely a manifestation of the cash nexus whereby all things must be measured in common coin, and that, with the overthrow of capitalism, we would simply enjoy those works which spoke directly to us – the only meaningful measure of their worth. Or maybe I'm just laying on you my own political naïveties, my ill-thought-out ideological maunderings.

Would we have liked each other? Odd that I should never have asked myself such a fundamental question. Would we even have had anything to say to each other; or would you have turned me to cinder with your scorn before I'd even strung two words together? I suspect you would. I never threw in my lot with the unremittingly righteous; and even if I had, they'd probably have been the wrong righteous from your point of view. It only took one misplaced phrase, didn't it, in those days, to mark someone without appeal as an enemy of the cause – even though the phrases we were using were scarcely distinguishable.

Who were you? That's what it comes down to. Who was the you who underlay all the news-flashes and the editorial trumpetings, all the bloated computer-files and cascades of punched tape, all the beer-stained cuttings, the recriminations, the malicious rejoinders, all the scraps of your own prose scissored and pasted, travestied by translation and selected to make someone else's point, and again these defaced and debased and abused photographs – the you who preceded it and the you who bore the weight of it? Who was the you I would have known if I'd known you? That's what I'm really asking. The you I would probably not have felt I knew at all.

If I get it right, it will answer me. I mean: my objective is to arrive at a portrayal of you that will carry such weight of truth as to be ungainsayable, and whose answers will carry such conviction that I shall be compelled to believe them even though it may be argued I shall have set them in place myself.

And when that is done, I shall plant lettuces at the back. I must eat a lot of eggs and collect their shells... Lettuces. That's a promise to myself, and to you also: the re-entry into normality that you never made because you believed normality was compromised – which is true – and ought never to be enjoyed for a moment – which is false. And I'll devote my retirement to producing large brass sculptures of slugs for the tourist market.

I've curtained the window on the landing. I realised what it was. It reminded me of the window through which I watched Gilmour leave with nothing but his toothbrush and face flannel in a paper bag, dragging his jacket around him against the downpour.

Did you, when the time came, know how to do the job properly: how to tie a noose – a hangman's knot, as it's called – and where to place the knot before you fell? Gilmour did. He always prided himself on his expertise in small matters.

TWO

It was only six o'clock, but night had come like the shutting of a great, hasp-snecked bible on a drab lectern. The air was splintering with cold. Under the broken boards of the outside privy, the slugs were snug in their sheaths of slime. A sullen roar rose up, and a car's headlights splashed the once-white front of the house with libations of milk, swinging like an insane censer as it took the twists of the lane's approach. Petra, coming in from the kitchen, was just in time to register the sound's cessation, a metallic slam, the thud of boots and a peremptory thumping on the front door. Hesitantly she called out, "Who's there?" but the noise drowned her voice. Defying by an effort of will a sudden nervousness, she took a flashlight and went back through the kitchen and round to the front, where a seemingly crazed man was relentlessly hammering.

"Ah – hi there! Was beginning to think I had to rouse you from an alcoholic stupor – or worse..."

"That door doesn't open. You'll have to come in this way."

"Look, I've brought a few goodies for tomorrow – have you got a fridge?"

"In this weather, you need a fridge?"

"There's a half a turkey, and some cranberries for sauce, and some chestnuts here to make stuffing with..."

"For tomorrow?"

"Petra, you do know it's Christmas, don't you?"

"Tomorrow – I hadn't quite realised."

"It's in all the papers – hot news – they're full of it."

"I don't take a paper."

"And the radio – when did you last listen to the radio?"

"A month or so ago, I suppose."

"Christ, you're looking thin. Are you looking after

yourself – eating properly?"

"You remind me of my mother. Just come in and sit down and I'll pour you a drink."

'Great. Well, then... Iechyd-da! Isn't that what you say in these parts? But honestly, poppet, you don't look unduly well."

"Oh, I eat – don't worry. Just that it's a bit of a limited diet. Two and a half miles to the nearest shop, so I think twice about going."

"Aren't there any buses into town?"

"Three times a week, yes; but it means staying there five hours. I've decided what I'll have to do is keep chickens. And grow lettuces. Can you live on just eggs and lettuce?"

"No; you need whisky as well. But eggs, lettuce and whisky – yes, that's generally acknowledge to be the perfectly balanced meal."

"Listen, it's nice of you to drop in on me like this."

"I had a high old time trying to find out where you were. I got hold of a phone number, but you seem to have been cut off."

"I have to be a bit provident these days."

"Well, you've certainly covered your tracks pretty well."

"It wasn't really a case of covering my tracks. I'd no reason to imagine anybody'd be interested in looking for me, that's all."

"Not a lot of visitors, then?"

"You could say that."

"Actually you did appear quite startled when you came out to let me in – as if you hadn't seen a living soul in months. Well, not so much startled as terrified. You ought to keep a dog, living in isolation like this. Didn't you and Gilmour use to have a dog?"

"Yes. Gelert."

"That's it – Gelert. What happened to him? He can't

have been that old."

'Had to be put down. Court order. Bit a kiddie in the street."

"I'm surprised. I remember him as a placid enough beast."

"He was a placid enough beast. God knows what the kid had done to provoke him – I wasn't looking when it happened – poked a finger up one of his nostrils, probably. But anyhow... It still makes my blood boil whenever I think of it. I mean, dogs have been taking nips out of children since the dawn of humanity. It's part of the deal. All right, a child may get scarred; but life's going to scar us all sooner or later, so why make such a fuss about it? But people don't think that way now. They think money. They think, 'My kid's been bitten by a dog. Great! How much can I squeeze out of that? A nice holiday, perhaps; trade in the car for a pricier model. Astonish the neighbours with my enhanced life-style...' So the bastards sued. And we lost."

"So how much did they take you for?"

"A fiver, as it happened – nominal damages. By the time the court got around to assessing it, the scar had faded almost to invisibility, and the child couldn't even remember which side it had been on. But I had to pay costs, of course. And give up Gelert. That was the painful part. Waiting our turn in the vet's waiting room. It crossed my mind you had to queue up to die..."

"You went in with him?"

"Yes. It was the last thing I wanted; but when a dog's invested all that trust in you... So I stood there stroking his head while some slip of a student in a white coat injected him in a vein with – what would it have been? – potassium chloride? I don't know. I didn't ask. It'd be nice to be able to say he raised his eyes to give me one last look; but actually he didn't. He seemed at first a trifle irritable with the inactivity – didn't know why we were all just standing around. Then his head sagged a little. Then it sagged again... It was all over in about half a minute. A perfect metamorphosis: living, responsive creature into inanimate limp bulk."

"Shite!"

"Yes. Still, how about you? I haven't even asked. Are you still with...?"

"Edward? Edward. No. Afraid he departed the scene nearly two years ago. I needn't tell you what with. It got quite messy in the later stages – what we'd once have called a bodily fluids piece."

"So did you... I mean, you nursed him through to the end?"

"Why wouldn't I have done? If you could do it for a dog..."

"I didn't mean anything... I asked because I didn't know. Simple as that."

"Yes. Simple as that. Oh, I'm sorry – it's just that it's all still pretty close to the surface."

"We both need another drink."

"There's quite a *déjà vu* for me about this place. I had a dream recently about a farmhouse where I was being made welcome: one of those dreams that stay with you for no obvious reason. There was a big easy-chair, tatty but comfortable, and one of those shallow stone sinks that'd only hold about an inch of water, and there was a nest of kittens somewhere that kept skittering about. And somehow those things added up to an atmosphere of – well, wellbeing."

"Amazing. Except for the sink and the easy chair and the kittens, I'd say you'd got it exactly right."

"Actually I think the dream came from somewhere I

once stayed with Robin. You won't remember Robin, do you?"

"Don't think so. Was he one of our bunch?"

"No, but he was a painter of sorts – struggling, needless to say. Easel stuff, basically. Worked a lot with pastels, and specialised in portraits and landscapes. I used to get rather miffed that he never did portraits of me; but he told me his landscapes were portraits of me. And perhaps he meant it, at that, because when I started to drift away from him – I'd met Edward on the course – it was his landscapes that changed: became violent, frenzied, angry. He started making broad strokes with the sides of the crayons, attacking the paper. You couldn't recognise any more what was being represented – except the anger. Then he went a stage further, into what he called 'given colour'. He'd flatten empty drinks cans and nail them to board, quite crudely, deliberately crudely, chunky and overlapping; but he still insisted these were landscapes, no more, though at the same time he clearly expected them to carry the freight of the self-loathing he'd invested in them. Ironically, the things achieved a certain popularity. For a while, his work sold comfortably well. But I was never entirely persuaded. The expressionist option can be very seductive. 'If I'm desperate enough when I do it, the work will embody the desperation.' All a hint too easy; and I'm just not sure it's true."

"I notice you're looking around you as you say that."

"Verily. *La lutte continue* – I'm glad to see it."

"I'm glad you're glad. But all that you were just telling me about your ex-boyfriend's work – was that meant to be some sort of a side-swipe at what I'm doing?"

"Well, I can't help noticing what I'd identify as a certain *tachiste* tendency. That sheet of paper over there – you seem to have been throwing plaster at it. And that clay head – if it is a head – is looking decidedly pummelled and scarred."

"We had a rule – remember? – No comment on work in progress."

"You did ask."

"You provoked me into asking."

"Only with monumental delicacy."

"I noticed. But all right, no, you're on the wrong track. I'm not interested in transferring the immediacies of my emotion to the materials. My own emotions are neither here nor there. Not that I haven't had to have that one out with myself; but I'm satisfied it really isn't about that. It's more a question of experimenting with textures, with surfaces, looking for something that will surprise me, perhaps – certainly for something that'll exceed the bound- aries of the sort of equivalences I've always taken for granted between the mark, or even the gesture that made the mark, and the thing the mark is geared to representing. And I suppose, underlying all that, there's a sort of act of faith – faith in the idea that, when the thing really does surprise me, it will surprise me for the right reasons."

"And those reasons?"

"Don't push me too hard, OK? This is likely to come out sounding mystical; and it isn't. It isn't at all. It's just that I haven't yet verbalised it in a satisfactory way – because, to be quite honest, I haven't tried, it hasn't seemed impor- tant."

"And because there's been no-one around for you to verbalise it to – or for. And that's understood. So tell me now, what is it that might come out sounding mystical?"

"It's the idea – the hope – that when it does surprise me, it'll be because I've got it right; and when I say 'got it right,' I mean I'll recognise her in it; which is to say I'll recognise it as embodying some truth about her which, although undoubtedly I'm the one who's put it there, will be a truth

I didn't know I possessed until I saw my own work, because I'd never before succeeded in articulating it. It'll be like seeing her face for the first time. So there it is. You'll probably tell me I sound like some Italian schoolgirl who can't wait to see a statue of the Madonna weep tears of blood."

"Please! Am I such a fearsome inquisitor? You're making perfect sense to me. I do sometimes wonder, though, about the value we set on the human face. Not that humanity's ever been unaware of the pitfalls – think of Macbeth. But all the same, it struck me with particular force just recently. There's been a flurry of news – I'm sure you won't have read it – I mean, it's the sort of thing you'd have disdained to read even when you did still take a newspaper – a flurry of news stories about a society divorce: this former model who'd married an aristo – and I don't mean 'model' in the red-lights-in-the-window sense, but a woman who'd prowled the catwalks in outfits of toadskin shagreen and minced buttercup and paper-clip chain-mail backed with camel felt..."

"You're making it up."

"I'm embellishing. That's allowed. So as I say, she'd married this aristo for his money – why else? – I've no problem with that – but the photographs that were appearing in the papers put a curious twist on it, because she had really quite remarkable looks, and not remarkable in the way you'd expect. It seemed a surprisingly genuine face: no visible make-up; no surgery to remove the wrinkles of experience; a little fold of flesh under the eyes whose precise angle seemed to say, 'I acknowledge you fully, because in so doing I acknowledge myself.' Just the sort of woman I'd enjoy having a long, relaxed natter with. Then, when it came to the settlement, it turned out that the things she most wanted, most valued, were the villa on the coast, the Silver Shadow, the interest-free platinum card at

Fortums, the polo team in its entirety: in a word, the dross."

"Hang on, though: you can't say it's all right to marry for money and then describe the things money buys as dross."

"Yes I can. It's one thing bleeding the rich, but you don't have to take on their value-system. There's room for a bit of ironic detachment."

"Fuck ironic detachment. No, I mean it. If the human face signifies nothing, doesn't that nullify at a stroke all human interaction – not to mention generations of pictorial art? Even dogs and cats look into our eyes when they want to judge our intentions. And that's not at all the obvious thing to do. You'd think it would make more sense to scrutinise our hands – see if we were carrying a whip or a tin-opener."

"I was only saying..."

"I don't think it was at all a bad idea, that rule against commenting on work in progress..."

"OK, point taken."

"Or perhaps even work completed. That's how I killed Gilmour."

"For heaven's sake, Petra, you didn't kill Gilmour. It was the system..."

It was like a pistol shot breaking a window pane. The shards tinkled to all corners of the room. A spillage of whisky on her shoulder and on the floor behind her marked the arc as she had drawn back her arm for the throw. The glass's thick base rattled nervously a few times, then desisted. It was as if a tap had turned off. Her hand trembled. Slowly she reached for the bottle and took a swig.

"I repeat: you did not kill Gilmour."

"Then I'll tell you how it happened, and you can tell me if I killed Gilmour. He'd been working on these studies for a still life. Somehow still life had always been his thing, even when he went through that phase of doing reliefs in aluminium mesh – they were still really still lives. Who knows where the sources of our compulsions ultimately lie? Anyhow, he'd been doing these studies, and finally he called me in to see the finished oil painting. It was fruit and vegetables bedded in a few grasses: all local produce – I mean nothing exotic – apples, blackberries, plums, parsnips, carrots... To be honest, I wasn't sure what to say. It was well enough executed; but somehow almost academic, even bland. I wasn't sure what the point was. And then Gilmour said, 'You do understand, don't you? You do know? I mean, all that stuff's genetically modified in one way or another.' And I said, 'How can you tell? We don't know. It's not labelled, is it? I seem to remember reading they've rigged the law so it's illegal to label it.' And he said, 'So what does that do to the painting?' I said, 'You can't tell anything from the painting;' and he said, 'Well exactly. That's the point. Can't you see? It's made a nonsense of it – a nonsense of painting. Nowadays something looks like a blackberry, but may for all we know be something genetically remote from a blackberry, or merely cognate with it. By calling this canvas 'Genetic Engineering', I'm drawing attention to the futility of our efforts. Painting has been rendered meaningless.' At that point I became a little impatient, and said, 'Jesus, has post-modernism really gone so far that all we can do is make perfectly crafted paintings to show the meaningless of painting? Wouldn't we be better off doing something we actually do believe in – or, failing that, nothing? Come back, Zhdanov, all is forgiven!' I heard a couple of doors slam. I looked out of the window and saw him walking away with a paper bag in his hand, dragging his jacket around him against the rain. He'd taken just his toothbrush and his face flannel. Within a couple of weeks, he'd hanged himself."

"He'd what? Look – and please don't throw that bottle at the wall, there's a dear – but the way I heard it, Gilmour didn't hang himself. He died of pneumonia. Are you saying everyone's been telling me porkies?"

"One story's as good as another. Perhaps mine simply helps me cope better. Takes a little of the weight off me. The weight of blame. He knew how to tie the knot, you know – the hangman's knot. Told me his scoutmaster had shown him when he was a boy."

"That at least I can believe. But there's a background to this whole business which I may be able to help sketch in for you – perhaps ease your mind a little. Way back, when we were still students – I used to chat to Gilmour quite a lot at that time – there'd been all that clamour from the sisters about the classic female nude, saying you couldn't paint a nude without raising issues of sexuality, and that if you tried to deny the sexuality it was even worse; and people had stopped painting nudes altogether because they couldn't handle the complexities – the ideological complexities, that is – and by the time we came on the scene, that was a bit old hat, so people were looking for ways to adapt that manner of argument with the aim of adopting a similarly unassailable moral position, and they'd begun to look at still life and say, 'Well how can you paint a still life as if it were just an exercise in line and pigment? You have to ask who planted and harvested all that nosh, what rates they were paid, what their living conditions were, how much surplus value was extracted from them...' and so on and so forth."

"And you're saying you think that was all nonsense."

"No, I don't think it was all nonsense, any more than the women's thing about nudes was all nonsense. But what I do think is that when your critical apparatus outstrips your creative apparatus, you're in trouble. You need both in balance – which means a certain amount of give and take.

Gilmour couldn't handle it. I saw him not handling it. I watched him fall to pieces. He took refuge in those quasi-abstract metallic things – which I actually thought were rather good – but the critics hounded him even there: 'An evasion of the pressing issues of exploitation of which his chosen subject-area is the ineluctable locus...' You know the sort of thing. So finally he settled on the idea of a painting not really being about what it was about, and that was the point of it because it was post-modern, and if you didn't see the point of it, then the more fool you. It had a lot more to do with that than with genetically modified parsnips, honestly it did – or at least as much. His last works were an attempt to duck out from under himself. He was trying to make the most of his weaknesses, just as we all have to – because most of us wouldn't get far relying on our strengths."

"All right: you're telling me he'd been painting from despair. But I'd questioned the validity of that despair. What could be worse?"

"From what you've said, you made a perfectly legitimate point which might just as easily have brought him to his senses. I don't even think they've produced any genetically modified parsnips or blackberries as yet. It's as I was trying to tell you: the system killed him."

"How come?"

"Because the invincibility of the system breeds intransigence in its opponents – just like your lady in the steel tower here."

"If you weren't an old comrade, I'd never let you get away with an argument like that."

"Well, he was an old comrade too. And I miss him. Remember how he used to throw down his brushes in mock exasperation and say, 'Roll on, Christmas; let's have some nuts'?"

"He also used to say, 'Roll on, death; demob's too far away.' Look, how about a short walk – just round the field at the bottom of the lane? There aren't likely to be sheep in it at this time of year."

"Of course, it's sheep country. Are they cloned, by any chance?"

"I haven't asked them."

"Sheep are supposed to recognise their own lambs by their bleats, you know – or is it the other way round? – even in an over-crowded field. Once they're all cloned, I suppose, they'll all sound alike. Just think of the muddle-ment at suckling-time!"

"Don't tell me you have an ethical position on sheep-cloning."

"Not an ethical one; but I find the aesthetics decidedly naff."

"I'll buy it. What are the aesthetics of Dolly the sheep?"

"Well, obviously, if you look at her as an example of human interference in natural processes, then there may be ethical questions to be asked. But if you look at her as a human artifact – which she undoubtedly is – a work of sculptural representation, then she's surely the last word in the lamentable progress of hyper-realism."

"Good point. In fact maybe you've succeeded in defining the crux at which artistic realism and political control become inseparable."

The moon, glimmering as if with rime, was the only thing to moderate the grim insistence of the stars. Cushioned under the undulations of frost-glittering grass and crunchy-cold sheep droppings slept living creatures whose pulses throbbed fast or slowly – foxes and rabbits, badgers, moles and voles – a graveyard of the living who lived off their own fat and planned for futures which might never come, fearful of each other, but fearful more profoundly because uncomprehendingly of the footfall of that predator who had raised predation to the plane of the metaphysical. Far above, untwinkling, a satellite bored its way through the constellations like a bacterium, harbinger of that plague which, if ever it should grasp the technology, our species will unleash upon the galaxy, looping and rooting from one inhabited planet to the next, to leave all life-forms squirming and shrivelled as salted slugs or napalmed babies. The heavy trees were ready to fall. A moon-faced owl sat motionless on a branch, then released itself softly onto the air to skim away fluff-mute and spectral.

"There are still owls here?"

"You see them once in a while. Better watch out on these tussocks. You can turn an ankle all too easily while you're looking up at the stars."

"It's God knows how long since I've seen so many."

"Where do slugs go in winter? Do they hibernate?"

"I don't think so. I think it's snails that do and slugs that don't. Why?"

"I'm going to have to collect egg shells if I want to grow lettuces."

"Eh?"

"Egg shells. They don't like crawling over them, so I'm told."

"I'm surprised. Someone said to me once that a slug's slime's so viscous it can crawl over an upright razor blade without cutting itself. I've always thought that a rather enviable talent."

"I sometimes have this vision – it'll come to me in a dream, though I think it's based on something that did actually happen once in a train, or perhaps the front seat on the top deck of a bus – of moving forward with a sort of exhilaration, a sort of ecstasy, into a night full of stars."

"What is it about stars? People only have to look at the Milky Way to start coming over all transcendental – thinking about human destiny, consciousness, free will..."

"I remember you had a very good theory about free will. You used say it was transparently nonsensical, but at the same time it was a necessary fiction, because there was no way we could act upon the assumption that we didn't possess it. That's stuck with me all these years."

"I'm impressed. Yes. But recently, what with all this Darwinism that's so much the rage these days, I've been turning my intellect to the question of consciousness."

"And you've evolved a Darwinian theory of consciousness."

"Bright girl! I won't wait to be asked. It goes like this. Either consciousness is a mere by-product of cerebral processes – I mean, an inevitable by-product, so that you couldn't have all the data-processing without consciousness being thrown up – 'emerging', I think is the word they use..."

"Or it isn't."

"Precisely. Or it isn't. Now then: if it is an inevitable concomitant of the function, then I have to believe that my desktop computer, even my pocket calculator in some perhaps very rudimentary sense, is conscious. Which is absurd. Or if not absurd, at any rate something I'm not prepared to swallow. Of course, you could argue that consciousness only happens when the machinery is organic – that's to say, carbon-based. But that seems to me a rather desperate manoeuvre."

"This is beginning to sound like a theorem with the QED at the start."

"Bear with me. If my calculator isn't conscious, that means – and this is where the Darwinism comes in – that consciousness must have evolved as a separate component of mental life, something not necessary but valuable in its own right – valuable to survival – even a dog's level of consciousness: it must have something to offer that the computation alone doesn't."

"And that something: you think it's free will?"

"I've always had difficulty with the notion of free will. It's always seemed so obvious to me that everything I do, everything I think, is the outcome of something I've formerly done or thought. In order to exercise free will, in any sense with a point to it, I'd have to do something – or think something – that nothing in my previous development had pre-disposed me to do or think: something I had no inclination of any kind to do or think."

"The surrealist *acte gratuit* – is that it?"

"No, that doesn't get around it: because first of all you have to have been motivated to be a surrealist."

"So in that case... You've lost me. If consciousness has some survival value independent of the processes it's conscious of, yet it isn't free of its own past, then what is it actually doing? Or put it this way: can a thought shift a molecule?"

"You're asking me? I've not the slightest idea. The theory's in its infancy. No comment on work in progress. But I do actually think it has to be something about being able to lay out all the options before ourselves. It may not be free will, but it gets us beyond simple species conditioning. And I'd guess that has to be a feature of anything we'd recognise as an intelligence, anywhere in the universe. The guys who wrote the Book of Genesis saw that, in their own way, and registered the shock of it. Just think: all options eternally available. On every inhabited planet of every one of those stars, somewhere there's an iron gateway with 'Arbeit Macht Frei' hammered over it by some brawny blacksmith dedicated to the New Order."

"What a lovely thought for Christmas!"

"Sorry, poppet. I was forgetting I came here to cheer you up."

"By the way, I'm afraid you'll be sharing your bedroom with a bicycle."

"But I adore bicycles! I envy the saddles the weight of their experiences."

"You haven't changed, have you? Still ready to camp it up when the going gets tough."

"There are worse ways of dealing with what life has on offer."

"I know. I've tried most of them."

Next morning he managed, after a few tentative tugs, to wrench open the door of the electric oven and sent a fine cloud of rust-motes billowing into a stray sunbeam. With patience he coaxed the appliance into life, and spent several hours turning the hunk of turkey and some scavenged vegetables into a positively Dickensian repast for a family of two. When it was over, they pulled a couple of crackers, read out to each other the silly jokes and sat chatting happily in their paper hats like a pair of Cecil Collins fools. At one point she said to him, "I'm glad you came. It's been good to talk together as we used to do in the days when we thought the world might benefit from our talking." Then he laid his hand on hers and said gently, "Don't destroy your-self, Petra. We've already lost too many of us. There are people back there, in the land of the living, who still care what happens to you. Let the dead bury their dead." It was as good a conclusion as can be hoped for.

THREE

Spank, spank, spank of the charcoal stick against the paper clipped to the small board I can rest on my knee against the window ledge.

It was good to see him; but I'm glad he's gone.

Charcoal: sticks o' willow, fossil twigs complete with knots. Black with a silver-satin sheen – bloom of a grape. Harshly chafing the coarse surface. Tooth, they call it.

Can make you see things afresh, just someone else seeing them – even if they don't say anything. Especially if they don't say anything, because then there's no resistance. So now my great white sails loom over me like rugged, rutted landscapes, geologies seen from the air, glacier-sculpted, paper fluffed up and smoothed again: gouged with charcoal and furrowed with chalk and morained with plaster – wounds bandaged with sized scrim. They're banners fit for an Act of Faith, dark as if smeared with the smoke from Inquisitorial fires. Does your face peer out from them? There's no knowing.

Icons of a brainy saint.

But even if he's right that a face means nothing, that's not to say that the image of a face means nothing: the image born of cthonic effort... That's what I ought to have said to him.

He brought it all tumbling back to me; and I've remembered things. Gilmour, before the confrontation with the infamous painting, tub-thumping on about, "How can you represent something whose difference is not evident because it precedes it?" and me not having an inkling what he was talking about, and him saying, "For all time till now, an object has stood for its essential properties, which we perceived as proper to it, natural to it, specific to it in the sense in which 'specific' relates to 'species'. All through history, we've been able to paint things in the knowledge that their appearance was somehow unique to their nature, was in some sense a guarantee of their identity. Now we don't know what's what any more. The apple we paint represents not the aeons-long evolution of apples, and of those of us who eat apples, but an electron microscope and an array of infinitesimal pipettes. And behind that, nothing: time eradicated." That's it, I remember: he was using this as a stick to beat my 'organo-symbolic' stuff with: "What value remains in the visual arts when a thing's nature no longer correlates with its appearance? Metamorphosis in art is effective because it's impossible, therefore shocking. Whether playful or profound, it's a defiance of taxonomy. But what price metamorphosis when all shape is untrustworthy from the root up?"

Perhaps that's why I withdrew to this backwater where nature's still more or less as our grandparents knew it. Not even a pylon visible from my windows. A place of respite, a retreat within which I could function for a while: for as long as I shall need, probably. But it's true the time is coming when there'll be nothing in the world that isn't tailored to our will.

And immediately I hear you say, "Our will? Whose will? Who do you mean by 'us'? Who benefits? You're not telling me it's for the universal good, are you? Which class owns the patents, and which is the excluded, the expropriated?" The charcoal crumbles like something that's been dead too long. And I remember a phrase he used: "Your lady in the steel tower." That's something that's been missing: an attention to your circumstances.

I was trying to carve a block of glass, a cubic block of glass, with a point and mallet, and glass was flying everywhere, and I thought it was because I couldn't get the angle of impact right, then someone whispered in my ear, kindly, braving the splinters, that it would only work if the point too was made of glass. "Diamond cut diamond, as people used to say." So what was that all about? Only purity can control purity, let alone shape it? But purity is something I've never aspired towards, because if I did I'd probably be dead too.

I've always had a fancy for improbable materials, ever since I was a child making little animals out of milk bottle tops. Perhaps I should.

He'd nursed Edward to the end. I didn't know that. Out there under the stars he said, "Perhaps we look at things the wrong way round. Perhaps what's truly astounding is that goodness should exist at all." I offer that to you as a simple piety; like the Christmas cards your children sent you in your steel tower; which you sent back unopened.

The music ambles amiably down imaginary streets: a headless, tailless worm of improvisation pursuing its endless evolution: great segments of time dropped from this continuum to live alongside life: the Cologne concert, the Paris concert, the Las Vegas concert... cassettes that have lost their boxes and lie among the plaster dust and charcoal flakings. Gilmour never liked Keith Jarrett: "That ever-spooling ribbon of private encephalography," he used to grumble. But I've lost my taste for things with beginnings, middles and ends. Ends, especially. Gilmour was wrong; hugging his shirt of Nessus, vanishing into the rain. Was wrong.

Do I turn to your death because I fear to dwell upon his? Forget it. There are some questions that should not be asked; and we know ourselves by finding out which these are. I see a hollow stainless steel cube, highly polished inside and out; and at the dead centre you hang, twisting slightly, from a wire invisibly thin. Perhaps that's what the dream was telling me. It was the cube that counted, not the glass.

★

The only logic of your actions was to dramatise the repressive relation of the state towards its population. That was all there was to it. To inscribe the system in your own experience and display it for all to see. That was the tactic developed by Bossmann from a few tattered tracts of Lenin and the unexpurgated aphorisms of Mickey Mouse. Bossmann the car freak, the petulant baby you all adored. Yet where was the sense of it? If the public didn't care when the police gunned down unarmed demonstrators while the man who gave the orders luxuriated in a performance of Don Giovanni – a detail worthy of Eisenstein, that! – what in heaven's name made you think they'd jump to the barricades when the authorities retaliated against people who actually were throwing bombs at them? So far as anyone knows, you weren't under secret instructions from the CIA – not like the Italians. But you didn't care. You had your dream. It was a dream in which people died – except that when you woke up, they stayed dead. The logic had taken over. Bossmann had taken over.

Inside a room of polished steel, featureless, muffled images endlessly reiterated, stuttering, progressively diminished, endlessly fading, having identity only in the sense of being identical... Thinking of you, I find myself in a room with no doors, and I look around perplexed: how can there be a room with no doors; and if there were, how could I be inside it? That was something you'd worked hard to achieve, and I have to salute you for it. You'd not appreciate my efforts to reclaim you for humanity. That was the last thing you wished. Humanism was bourgeois, contaminated, complicit. Only to be hated by all, even those working for your release, could deliver you from its taint. Am I getting warm?

Weld the stainless steel, then. Shut the lid before your essence escapes. But no. You can't hang yourself in a stainless steel cube. Walls smeared with hand gropings; as hands smear mirrors, as lips smear mirrors, as exhaustion smears mirrors. Inaccessible as crystals in a closed vug.

Where did I begin? What did I want from you? Was there something I wanted to know about myself, perhaps? Discount store psychiatry! At first it seemed – didn't it? – purely technical: to reconstruct a face from its bruising: to reverse time: to erase the traces of error... But then you have to ask, what error? And whose? Coming across my Buchenwald studies, I remembered the doubts, the need I felt to identify with the world's sufferings, the knowledge that I couldn't, the hope that the materials would do it for me if I handled them properly. And you, too, knew you couldn't: not enough; not to satisfy you; and for you there were no materials but your own being.

An image I saw once; a photograph from one of the camps: a bunk woven from barbed wire. There was nobody in the picture; but I couldn't help visualising the black-suited lads with heavy protective gloves stringing it, threading it, all a big laugh, then forcing some elderly, patient pastor to lie on it in his worn camp pyjamas: "All right, then, Grandpa – comfy, are you? Have a good night's sleep, then..." Why am I thinking these things? This was never meant to be a meditation on human brutality; and they'd never have done such things to you, much as you wanted to play up your own victimhood – not even if they ended by killing you, as some believe. Were you perhaps bowed down under the hard, dread weight of what your parents' generation had done – even though your own parents had certainly had no part in it?

My bed-linen is rotting. There's no launderette within miles, I'd have to wash it in the bath, and there's no way I could get it dried in this weather. It'll have to wait till spring.

Generalisation is no way to proceed.

Your cell. I must try to be specific. I imagine it in ribbed steel, oppressively hygienic, with perhaps just room for a tubular steel chair between the bunk and the wall, and a steel shelf that hinges down for you to eat on and write on. Would they have let you have a laptop with you? Well of course not! One forgets how long ago it all happened. The computer on which the police cross-referenced all your friends and movements would have been a bulky old mainframe, doubtless programmed in one of those cryptic, acronymic languages that sounded like patent-protected petroleum derivatives.

What is on my bathroom shelf? A battered pack of elastoplast; a roll of copper shim; nail clippers; two pairs of earrings and a necklace in a little ceramic bowl which once held pâté; a jar of cocoa butter because my hands get terribly chapped this time of year, especially when I'm working with clay... So what would be on yours? A school exercise book bearing the insignia of the Republic? A mug containing two prison issue pencils but nothing to sharpen them with? A pair of glasses? A grater for the hard skin on your heels? A hairbrush? A nailfile? Eyebrow tweezers? Tools to shape yourself for the world... Yes, your writing materials above all. But does the prison-pencil falter in your hands once in a while? Do you doubt your analysis when you see that everything has become circular, self-confirming, and do you want to escape that, yet see no path but the ever-tightening inward spiral? But I said no generalisations. So you pace your small space, four steps forward and two sideways, then back; and then there would be the routine searches, the indignities, the pettiness, the intimate probings, the antiseptics and prophylactics; and bath-time, always under supervision. Your kin were men of the cloth. I find it impossible to imagine you naked. Yet the guards must have seen you.

How do we measure victimhood? You had a radio in your cell; and a flush toilet. What then were you resisting; and how was your resistance expressed? The precise angle of an eyebrow, the precise torsion of the neck... Rip up another page and start again. Sinews of the Burghers of Calais – whose gigantic hands and feet, some say, were contributed by Camille Claudel. Vast crowds followed your coffin to the graveyard, and most of those people were sure you'd been murdered. Their reasoning? That you, the great analyst, would not have killed yourself without leaving behind a devastating critique of the developments of which this was simply the latest twist, the game in which this was simply another move: the suicide note as weapon in the struggle. To me, the lack of a note was the measure of your despair. A final self-laceration.

What would you say to me if we were to meet? I can guess. You'd ask me how I dared question your contribution to the progress of socialism. You'd ask me if I thought my spoilt-child, self-indulgent dabbling in mud pies and sooty smudges was contributing to the betterment of society. Probably not, I'd say; but at least I'm still here, kneading the dough of the world. I haven't displaced it behind an abstract calculus of exegesis and gesture.

Oh please don't tell me I don't understand the message. It's that the power of the authorities is so arbitrary that it can be opposed only by manifestations of equal arbitrariness. All justification is complicity, because it accepts their definitions of justice. The formalities can go hang. It's not the banality but the fatuousness of the evil that demands rejoinder. Can I pass, friend, and be recognised?

No, it's true: we'd probably not have got on. I've never been at ease with fanatics. Yet it's almost as if you were trying hard to be a fanatic and never quite succeeding: a failed fanaticism; and the knowledge of this failure tore you apart. Why did you want it? Just to be in Bossmann's good books? That's scarcely credible.

You'll say you couldn't have backed out. Of course you could. You could have served your term, doubtless inflated by your refusal to testify against your former comrades, and you could have weathered their scorn – which you tried to weather anyhow, and which drove you to your death because you couldn't disengage from them...

There are no photographs of you smiling.

Scarring the face again with cross-hatching, the enlargement so big it scarcely registers as a face within the width of the room – and that is what I wanted, to have to copy shapes without their collapsing back into the signification of a glare or a grimace. Whether to start with plaster yet: to slop it wet, to slice it dry, to mummy it with soaked muslin. I've built up more clay than the armature was meant for. Clay the consistency of a punchbag. But I've neglected to keep it moist; and chunks have dropped off leaving interesting surfaces. The lines on my hands are like ravines from long handling of abrasive substances: maps of the underground waterways of abandoned cities. The clay surface, geological almost; glacier-scarred almost; reminds me of something – what? – no, I've lost it.

Milky puddles in the grey light. The wind shuddering

and thumping in the chimney... Let's say your politics mean nothing to me. It's only your face I care about. Can we establish that as the basis for an honest relationship? Mutual respect? Your bone-structure buried under the swellings. The eyes peering out defiantly; uncertainly; resentfully; uncomprehendingly; dourly; blankly... No, I forbid myself to conceptualise you, think of you in words. It must be the pencil and the spatula only: trust to the primal intuition of the image: of Lascaux; of the Willendorf Venus.

A pigeon was perched on the roof ridge, its head hunched into its shoulders as if it were mimicking a bird of prey. In fact it was cold. The tiles were white with frost, though it was already ten o'clock in the morning. And the sky behind the bird was peach-coloured; which is to say that it was composed of all the colours of a peach, from buff yellow through brick red to purple.

That is something I saw one day from the window of our drawing office, which was on the top floor of a building in Bloomsbury. It's a scene I've never forgotten. It filled me with an indescribable happiness: a feeling which its recollection, all these years later, can still faintly stir into being. It is one of those moments, like the Welwyn viaduct, which come to mind whenever I begin to muse upon the relation of visual experience to life in general.

We don't get delicate peach skies here. Not enough pollution, I dare say.

Some years after I gave up the job, I ran into one of my old colleagues in a supermarket, and she asked me if I remembered Miss Jardine. Of course I did. She'd been a tracer there as long as anyone could remember. A good deal older than me. All the same, she hadn't seemed to resent it when I was promoted above her – or at least, never showed it, never took it out on me. Anyhow, it seemed that Miss

Jardine had finally retired, and, taking with her some tacky goodbye present which she evidently treasured, gone to live in a bungalow somewhere in Essex – Laindon, I think it was. Two years later, she'd died of cancer. Alone. No friends. "She'd given her life to the company," was how my informant put it. Perhaps that's why, once I began to feel a funny numbness in my left arm from time to time, I decided to pack up and come out here where I'd be on my own. Can that be true? Is that how our motives work? A warped sense of deference to a dead woman I never particularly cared about?

Not that it matters. It's the sort of story people are always telling one another; and, by telling it, they somehow neutralise it into that ritual sadness of two people commiserating in the dusk while smoke drifts up from the chimney pots to sneak across a red sun. Or that, at least, is how I remember it, impatient, waiting for my mother to finish chatting so that we could go home to tea. As a child, I did not understand this suppression of horror into formalised gestures of resignation, the woebegone murmur of disbelief, war-wives' stuff; and after every dutiful visit to aunts or uncles I came home desolated by the litanies of pain, sorrow, agony, trouble and loss. So have I the right to accept the story of Miss Jardine in its stripped minimalism, let alone to make it a pretext for action of my own in a wholly unrelated context? That, after all, is where I think it began for me: what I initially rebelled against: the way those stories were told. That was the kernel of my politics.

And what would have happened if I hadn't rebelled: if I'd accepted the assimilation of all things into a prior morphology, the lexical gestures of saints and martyrs on frescoes, the exact incline of the head that bespeaks sympathetic concern or outraged probity or maternal nurture; the narratives just waiting to be peopled by new characters as the old ones depart the stage, but never changing? As a female you're supposed to be intuitive, impulsive, even a trifle reckless but in the end quiescent. That was the script I was handed at the door. And if I'd lived my life as my friends were urging me? Well, they tell the story in their own persons: one a battered wife who eventually did away with herself; one a socialite of faded glitter trying to keep a foot-hold in the gossip columns by faking scandal; one whose children's addictions read like the lyric of a patter song; yet another who's on her fourth husband, each more affluent and indifferent to her than the last... Those are the dramatic ones; but then there was someone whose name I forget who married a farmer – I always think of the character in *The Waves* who went all staid and jam-making, clonking the caked mud from hubbie's boots at eventide... What would a farmer's wife be doing these days, I wonder? Cross-referencing the DNA of the breeding stock on a Macintosh, probably. Yet perhaps it was, again, this that brought me here. By 'this' I mean a response not to Miss Jardine's story as such but rather to the manner of the telling of it: the same move as I had made long before, but on a farther square of the chessboard. All the same, it has to be admitted that my former friends are out there among the multitudes while I stay nunnishly devoted to a single physiognomy in which I hope to find – what? – enlighten-ment? – salvation? No, just the intimation of another human presence buried, embalmed in history, denied speech.

I'm sorry. I've no right to make you take the burden of all this. For some time it's seemed to me that you may be my swan-song. My urgency, which may readily be mistaken for a compulsion to get the work finished, is in fact only a compulsion to get it right. And besides, you found your own solution. But for all that, nothing is inert.

They even say brambles feel pain when you hack them down; and I sometimes believe I hear them sobbing in the night. That is what defeats my understanding. That is why our eyes do not meet. If I had had your children, I would have protected them. I would have sat up by night-light through their coughs and fevers. I would have protected them. I would have protected them against storms, against the police, against the dialectic of history, against the free-will of the galaxies. I would have protected them against petty vengefulness and sublime obedience. I was capable of love.

Last night I dreamt of food: a stoneware bowl full of – well, I'm not altogether sure, but there were little new potatoes done in their skins, and perhaps roast parsnip, roast celery, all sprinkled with coarse-chopped herbs... It was the colours that mattered: all earth tones, ochres and sage. I don't think I experienced the taste in the dream; but the colours somehow stood for the taste, and I don't know how long it is since I've seen something so delicious. What food did they give you in prison? I don't even know that. Greasy sausage and mash on a tin plate? Probably not. It was a model establishment.

Jarrett's music is traversing a featureless landscape – so featureless, in fact, that you can scarcely tell it is moving at all. Then it hesitates, sniffs the air, and, with the yelp of a wounded weasel, modulates through a couple of crash-barriers into another reality.

It would help if I knew what sort of music you listened to in your steel chamber. Churchy stuff, at a guess – enjoyed with a touch of guilt. And did you perhaps enjoy the guilt more than you enjoyed the music? It wouldn't surprise me... But all this is conjecture.

I'll never succeed in approaching you through detail.

I can stand back. Stand back once more and think about it. No-one is pushing me; and there's always scope for reconsideration while we're still alive. Yes, it's true: I'm through with the time-orgasm: time as a progressive constriction, a narrowing of the focus to the one awaited moment when it will reach almost limitless intensity before diffusing again into a lazy whirl of seconds and minutes, and we find ourselves wondering what they're for as we adapt to the fact that the job's finished and it's time to be thinking about another. I suppose that's the key to all that sado-masochistic, *Tristan and Isolde* self-immolation which I've never understood – the link between sex and death. But the difference with death is you can't consider it retrospectively. If you're still alive, it must have been sex. To get back to what I was saying, though: was this a wise project in the first place?

'Wise' – ?

Your words still rant as they always did; but your comrades are not deceived. They discern the doubts that beset you. Why did we do all this? Yes, society is rotten and hypocritical, but what have we actually done to change it? Two years on the run; two years of the underground struggle, so-called: two years of feverish activity, car-chases complete with skids, ground-breaking invective, heists of small change from sleepy banks, louche disguises, fake hand-grenades cast in aluminium, Raffles-style purloining of official notepapers and seals – and for what? All this just to keep the organisation going, to pay for the food and the safe houses and the forged documents and the false number-plates and the endless trekking from city to city to keep one step ahead of the law. Aside from a couple of bombings in retaliation for Cambodia, after which you were all rounded up within weeks, what did you ever actually do? Not so much propaganda of the deed as propaganda of the two-reeler, Mack Sennett crossed with blood-and-thunder, give the authorities the run-around – we can all see the fun in that. More difficult, though, when you were obliged to continue the fight by other means, when your only medium was the legal process: challenges to the legitimacy of the court; earth-shattering declarations on points of order. Quick – another press release! Another chance to lay bare the machinery of oppression! Three years of it. And then, of course, the hunger strikes on this pretext and that. "Forced feeding is torture." Doubtless it is. And no-one breaks ranks. One man – I've seen his photograph – shrinks away inside his taut skin till he looks like someone excavated after a millennium or two in a bog. Oh yes, he's dead all right. Bossmann calls off the strike: Our point has been made; we must keep something in reserve. Some what? Some more of his comrades' lives, that's what. This doesn't feel much like the Keystone Cops.

Of course, all these decisions are meant to be democratic, arrived at after rigorous discussion and analysis. And you, being the most highly regarded as a thinker, must surely... But I've seen these small-group democracies. As often as not, they fall into thralldom to some masterful male to whom the women all defer and swing every vote in his favour. Bossmann, whose every sneeze picked a fight and whose every cough re-defined his authority... Is that really all it was about? Somehow I can't believe it of you – but perhaps that's simply because I don't want to believe it. Still, you weren't his mistress. Is that what you wanted, then? I doubt it. More likely it was the age-old, stereotypical dread of the inadequacy of the intellectual, a compulsion to ally yourself with someone capable of action, someone who might make a real difference in the world. Yes, obviously you would abide by group's decisions once they were taken; but as for subordinating your analysis to Bossmann's as a matter of blind love – no, it doesn't ring true to me. And perhaps the key lies in this.

Nothing has changed, yet nothing remains the same. An equilibrium has subtly shifted; and there is now one voice that lays claim to the identity of the whole. And you can't reverse the process – you know this – without destroying all you have created. So what of your own voice? Even your letters to your children betray a strange dislocation, as if you were trying to remember what a mother's letters to her children ought to sound like – "My dear little kittens, it does seem such a terribly long time since we saw one another..." – and are eventually abandoned because all human ties are suspect except to the group whom you have invoked, called up like shrouded assassins from the exhalations of a marsh, or whose association is gratuitous and therefore exemplary. Well, I can't deny there's something attractive in this – or if not attractive, at least sympathetic to someone without ties of her own, albeit less voluntarily or relentlessly so. But why such overwhelming joylessness?

I find that for the last few minutes I have been insistently battering the same lump of clay: a lump the size and shape of a child's boxing glove. We have arrived by our separate routes to confront each other alone in this stone cell. Your writing, of course, admits no reservations. But hairline fissures appear in it which do not pass unnoticed. You have not stopped thinking. And the trouble with thinking is that one can't always be sure where it may lead. The Revolution does not think; it knows.

The slugs are back. For a long time they've been submerged, travelling in loose convoy, a 'wolf-pack' as they say in war movies, communicating by sonar bleeps and pulses like someone in intensive care. But now they're back.

Last night they slid over me; and I felt the successive little tremors of coldness, reaching and shrinking, exploratory, as they crossed my breasts and my face, a big albino the colour of white chocolate slinking majestically between my thighs, seeking to enlarge the sphere of their experience. I must have been dreaming; but this morning, outside the kitchen door, I saw their sparkling, evanescent lithograms on the flagstones.

Perhaps I'll leave it as it is, unfinished. Destroy all the studies, destroy all that is completed, within its own limited terms, leave only this punished clay as monument to its own punishment – and mine – and yours. Let them think, when they find my desiccated body fallen beside that tentative and inexpressive bulk: Here was her masterpiece! There's nothing to match the eloquence of the unfinished work, especially when nobody'll be absolutely sure whether it is unfinished or not. I see it displayed in a white room, misted by a discreet spray; and someone will have rescued scraps of torn wash-drawings and charcoals from the trash bin, from among the vegetable peelings, and mounted them on framed acid-free board with all the care due to a flood-damaged Cimabue; and a little gadget with a clockwork drum will track the humidity with a red trace on graph paper, and the temperature in black; and this gadget will be incorporated into the installation, and one of the graphs will hang framed over a print-out of the cardiogram from my last heart check. And in a surgically white vitrine will be displayed, as a summation of my life, a decoy pigeon, a jar of pickled slugs, two jars of broken eggshells, a scattering of mysterious plaster starfish and a lettuce set in resin, all this against the background of a blue-print – a genuine blue-print, visibly creased where it's been folded and stuffed in the site engineer's pocket – of the Milky Way as seen from Mount Palomar. Do they still do blue-prints? I shouldn't think so.

★

The others are simply who they are. But you, in spite of all your efforts, remain someone to whom your own choices contribute; and, however impeccably you elaborate the implications of agreed doctrine, the others know this. Rapping of knuckles against steel walls transmits from cell to cell the rumour of your unreliability.

There is no longer any experience against which to measure theory, nothing to prevent the slogans from growing more and more baroque, narcissistic, ornate. It is only a matter of time before small differences swell to monstrous dimensions in a culture where it goes without saying that human sympathy is to be dismissed as indulgence.

The lonely cell, which for most prisoners is a crucible of madness, has become for you a refuge from that greater madness in which your three or four companions cease-lessly boost the ever-more-constricting circuit of your own thoughts to turn them back on you in scorn and loathing, casting you out with flaming swords from the territory of your belief. And Bossmann, too, isolated from human contact except for one half-hour per day spent belabouring his comrades for their laxness; banged up in solitary – soli-tary, that is, except for the endless stream of left-leaning lawyers who come to receive an update to their brief topped with a dollop of vituperation and to find in his insults a perverse beatitude, a conviction that they are less sullied by their professions than they had formerly feared. Oh yes, they grumble, to be sure: "We work our guts out for that bastard, and he's never grateful..." But then they remind themselves that gratitude is bourgeois, and depart feeling much the better for it. Ennobled, even.

And so: another hunger strike, just to keep the show on the road – the show being little more than the endless to-ings and fro-ings of state prosecutors, TV journalists, prison governors called to stuffy ministries; and the rag-bag army satisfied that actions were being taken – heroic actions? – no, heroism is bourgeois – just footling bouts of dialectical necessity from Bossmann's implacable oppositional will. And you? You'd hate me for talking like this, I know. Yet for you, who wanted to prove yourself rather than prove your devotion: all that seemed to remain for you was to sacrifice more and more of yourself. The only statement a denial, to be allegorised soon enough by the ultimate denial. Every suicide is a plea: 'Not guilty as charged.' But there again, who knows whether you may not have recognised this yourself and submitted it to scrutiny. Perhaps you saw, as the others did not, that fascism was not something you could localise, assign to the state or the police or the military exclusively; that it was present as a bacterium in our minds as in our society, present in your elevation of Bossmann to predominance even though you'd never been his acolyte, had done your own thinking, but had needed his urgency and certainty because true thinking can't fail to be accompanied by doubt and doubt seemed weakness, and now, with only the four of you, you feared his contempt because it would exile you from all meaning, from the source of meaning in your solidarity; and you couldn't take succour from the world outside, not even from your kids, because this was something you had to hunt down alone and extirpate, this fascism in yourself, this reliance on Bossmann not for analysis but for power, because without power evil cannot be overthrown, yet the power is the evil, has been tracked round and round into the tight spiral of its own contradiction from which there is no escape except...

This is not a face I have made. What is it? It is a rock and it is a chronicle.

In your death, as in some awful Greek archetype, a myth

to keep shrinks in gainful employment, you enacted our own contradictions. But you did not, for all that, escape them; did not expiate them; did not uncoil the spiral. It was the wrong answer. Yes, listen to me for a change: it was the wrong answer. You should have let the world in, have let your own children in – if only to teach them to anticipate the fascism within themselves, to know what was coming and be ready for it, to say to them, "I am your parent. Do not trust me. Do not trust anyone with power, even the power conferred by your own love of them."

But there, I've no evidence for any of that. And in any case, you wouldn't have listened to me. The more people tell you you're wrong, the more you can dismiss them; and the more people you can dismiss, the more pure you are. A sterility strangely consequent upon a passion for life. All I can feel sure about is that you went on thinking – a bourgeois thing to do – even when there was nothing left to think about but the need for ever more complete self-annihilation, for destruction – if only within yourself – of what made the world corrupt: in effect, of your own humanity. Beyond that, there remained only the sneers, the compulsive ganging-up that goes on in small groups when there's no-one to victimise but each other. It was all the way back to the school playground.

I can watch endlessly from the kitchen door as the mist evaporates between the ranks of pines: Hiroshige and his spiky glyphs. And there, far above where you think the ridge must be, the mist is illuminated by a vagrant sunbeam to delineate a grassy slope surrounded by trees of palest gold. It is the way a Victorian artist would have portrayed heaven. Slug Heaven – nearer the mark than Bryn Derwen. 'Heaven' is 'nefoedd' – I remember from all those hymns... Difficult to think spring's nearly here, with only a few tiny yellow blooms on something that looks vaguely like jasmine. But there are incipient shoots on everything if you look closely: hence the sense of a faint shimmer of green over that stand of birches on the edge of the field below. Any day now I'll be able to wash the sweaty sheets and, if they don't disintegrate in the process, hang them outside to dry. Spring cleaning. I begin to see what our parents saw in it. All that coal ash from the long winter to be washed from the paintwork and the beading; glassware to be polished up to catch the miserly sun. But it's not just that, it's something psychological. Those great soiled sheets of paper, gashed with the marks of cumulative desperation, shredded in places with excess of zeal, tearing under their own weight. A face that will never be a face. A woman who will never do the one thing I have wanted her to do: turn and smile at me. History looks drab the day after.

But... *La lutte continue*. It's not over yet. There's still work to be done.

It's true. It's not just a trick of the dawn. The paper looks at me in smuts and dregs: burnt wood; graphite; splashed ink. Blurs. Knife marks. Crossed lines of thorn thicket. Scars for mouth and eyes. No help: no reach of a hand into the dark where my hand waits to clasp yours. Stab of grey, stab of white, here and there a curve – so what? I was wrong to imagine I might surprise a smile from you this way, or even that that was the reason.

But one new line of approach has opened for me. It's struck me that I was mistaken to see despair in your last act. You wouldn't have killed yourself unless you'd had unbounded hope – a hope too big to bear, too hard to work for, too awful in its demands. How do I know? Because you wouldn't have done it today. No-one would. You'd have shrugged at the futility of action and settled for writing pornography or becoming a success in the fashion trade.

Suicide isn't worth committing if there's nothing against which to measure your desolation.

You exercised the final sanction. That is the source of your appeal, and also of your opacity.

So let it be plaster: a big head in plaster. Never mind the smile. A big white head with perhaps dark areas on the surface to indicate shadows at variance with the actual contours. Shadows of clouds on cliffsides. An exercise in contradiction. Or no, better still, have hoops of birch or hazel embedded in the mass, breaking surface occasionally to define orbits which appear and disappear again, conic sections, something to implicate the interior, the internal, the concealed. Forget likeness altogether, or have it secondary. The scaly old zinc bath to mix the plaster in...

Oh no! They took your corpse out in a zinc bath, didn't they. They drag it squealing along the steel treadplate of the catwalks, clanging it down the staircases... A hommage to Marat? Hardly. Do they cover you with a dust-sheet? Does your arm hang limp and pale?

You were never to know it, but the others followed your example not so long afterwards – yes, even Bossmann, though I'm sure he must have sneered with his last breath that you'd chosen an ideologically inopportune moment. So what happened? Did they finally tire of the game and want to go home to bed? Bossmann perhaps thought he could blow his brains out today and call a press conference tomorrow to expatiate upon the implications of it. But then Bossmann never did have much use for his brains. Too busy being decisive.

The piano – a strangely metallic sounding piano with galvanised bodywork – the piano is beating up to a triumph, seemingly three-handed, to the accompaniment of intermittent whoops and howls. But it won't end on triumph; it'll subside into a tormented uncertainty shortly before the last chord.

One of your associates testified to the court that, the evening before your death, you'd all spent a relaxed half hour discussing the nature of identity and consciousness. Perhaps that wasn't such a good idea... A man in a hip bath that salves his boils and draws their pus. Head at a sag. Mouth wide. Quill still lodged in the hand, write hand. One who writes till the knife has let too much blood...

Kick back.

Back kick. Back back kick.

Back.

Pain too cold too hard.

Chain off the gears. Kick. Kick.

Out of phase. Faint. Christ, what's wrong with me?

Get the chain back on the gears. No. Quiet. Calm down for God's sake and wait.

Wait.

Lens of a pince-nez all shards.

Who am I? It has torn out my name like a bad soft tooth.

Wait. It'll come back in time if you don't think about it.

And now they all clap like mad as the last notes die. Fade out. I can't have been here so long as it seems then.

I should have paid those phone bills. Too late to think of that now.

You're safe if you can stick it out for a full day I was once told – or is it two days?

Not sure.

Not sure of what?

Ought I to go up to bed? Is it safe to move? Daren't risk it. The floor's hard though and cold.

Down. Roll down.

All those things we knew. What a waste.

Who was I then? The back of my head hurts.

So how am I meant to eat? A frail flame from wax clasped in dead hands. 'For a bowl of borscht.' Small waves lap the blocks of the mole as the ship rides on a smooth swell.

Oh yes we all know the score. Why else do you think I've spent all this time with you?

The pram rocks on the edge. Quick sprag the wheel. We knew.

But the pram picks up speed as it jolts down the steps. The guard. Call out the state troops in white coats and black boots. Raise the guns. The crowd flee. Mute screams are heard. Shoot down the slope as they all rush for dear life a man with a crutch a boy with a torn coat a girl in a frock with lace trim. Smoke. Guns spit puffs and feet trudge down one step more. A man falls. More feet. A child. The swift sharp flash of a sword and a howl and a gashed eye.

Frame by frame so slow. It's just a film when all's said and done. Yet it still goes on and you took it to heart and were right to.

I knew it would come. It had to. And I would be there to. I would.

Still no name for me. But I dare say it's all to the good when push comes to shove. After all we don't set out in life with a name do we?

And we all wind down in the end too. Wind down like toys. Like tin cars and tin trains with flat keys that turn in jerks as they move till down to one last spasm. Was it like this for you? Bombs tracts thefts. What was it all in aid of? Two bad eggs don't make a good one as my Dad would have said. And that's not the half of it. And yet in the gaol's cold gut I search for you. In my dreams I peer in through the bars of your cell and find it void as they take you in a tin tub to stitch you in a hemp sack. Your hair your eyes your mouth your hands...

There's a shape I could not find and it is the shape you were. Must try once more to trace a path to your truth. There must be such a path for each of us. No? We each have our truth shut in a box like a cat. Don't say we don't.

The great white slug slides in my left ear and out of my right one. My brain is made of slugs that coil and seethe and slip and slew. Yes – they got in one night and bred. That is why I don't feel them pass through my skull. It's all right it does make sense. Of a sort. Sort of. Baa baa black sheep not what it used to be.

It's dark out there. The glass has the gleam and glint of boots shone black with a rib bone so smooth you can see your face in them – see your face as he knouts you. I must have been laid out a long while. Is it safe to stand up? No don't risk it yet. The end of a train of thought. All gone to pot. I can't bear that you see. The rhythm is back to front – still back to front though not so bad. It's just not right that's all. What would it take to jump the chain back on the cog? You'd think you could just – I don't know quite what.

The wind soughs in the trees and the leaves turn their pale sides to us all at once. Clouds flit white as death's fleet of barques in full rig. The crowd stand ghosts and shades brought by spilt dregs of wine from the far shore of the slow grey flood like peg dolls clad in rags to see you laid to rest in the birch grove. Each face which is pale too as birch bark and frowns in doubt forms words soft or harsh. Each knows it is too late an hour for new life to raise its hand and clench its fist in hope or cast a stone. Thus they wait tense and weak and watch with round owl eyes and the words they croak soft or harsh though hard to hear join up to weave a skein of black wool smoke which drifts and rolls thick to the lip of your grave and is drawn down to shroud or vex or grieve you and is seen no more. For each knows the signs must turn and twist with the leaves and fall. Will fall. Like leaves of books like psalms. And that is why a hush falls and they fade and are gone and only the dug soil is left a mouth to tell of you: a slit trench in a war with no end in sight. My war as it was yours though you'd not have seen it that way.

No name is safe and good.

With a thump a lump falls from the big clay head and leaves a flat plane rough. And all at once from down here I find the link I could not make till now. When I was three or four years old and to the south. On a trip with some aunts. A high hill. That's right. Tough climb for a child. The turf was soft but with hard shelves of stone. The wind came in gusts so strong they held my aunts' skirts tight to their shins to whip them like stiff flags as they went in front of me bright against the sky. Ah. Once in a while a sheep would bleat far off. Coarse grass bent with the wind and swept in broad bands. My small legs were tired. But then as we made our slow way up the slope a great rock rose from the lee of the ridge and it was huge and bit by bit I saw it rise so high that it took up all the sky I could see. Garn Fawr. They told me when we got home I had seen Garn Fawr. No sound. Not a bird – or if there was I did not hear one. No sound but the drum of the wind in my ears.

It spoke with no voice. A still world egg old as the sea and young as the sea or the sky is young. A vast weight. But a vast weight of peace. Great weight of calm. The light of a frail sun fell on its scarred face cracked by the sun's warmth for years and for years. And at once I knew it loved me. Knew it loved me more true than God. And though I did not call it back to mind for years and years it was still there though lost and out of sight.

I was a child. But that was the start of my life my worth my art.

Garn Fawr: the name has come home to me when my own has gone for good: the first true me of all.

A place to set out from and a place to come back to. Just that. And that's why: all the time your weight of love.

I'm cold. Cold.

Is it safe to get up yet? I can't stay here on the floor all night.

Blood sticks.

Blood sticks blood stones can break my bones but.

My hair's stuck to the stone with dry blood that tugs as I move.

Both my hands are numb.

I can't let the fire die down or I'll freeze to death. My feet are like ice as it is.

And there's not much food in the house.